Reading Power 系列

★ 多益英語測驗/全民英檢初/中級適用
★ 學科能力測驗/指定科目考試/統一入學測驗適用

Intermediate

英閱百匯

Let's Read Real-World English!

附解析本

車昀庭　　　　　審閱
蘇文賢　　　　　審訂
三民英語編輯小組　彙編

三民書局

 Reading Power 系列

英閱百匯

彙　　　編	三民英語編輯小組
審　　　閱	車昀庭
審　　　訂	蘇文賢
企劃編輯	陳逸如
責任編輯	謝佳恩
美術編輯	黃顯喬
內頁繪圖	李吳宏

發 行 人	劉振強
出 版 者	三民書局股份有限公司
地　　　址	臺北市復興北路 386 號 (復北門市) 臺北市重慶南路一段 61 號 (重南門市)
電　　　話	(02)25006600
網　　　址	三民網路書店 https://www.sanmin.com.tw

出版日期	初版一刷 2018 年 3 月 初版二刷 2020 年 7 月
書籍編號	S804540 4712780656563

三民書局

知識，就是希望；閱讀，就是力量。

在這個資訊爆炸的時代，應該如何選擇真正有用的資訊來吸收？

在考場如戰場的競爭壓力之下，應該如何儲備實力，漂亮地面對挑戰？

身為地球村的一分子，應該如何增進英語實力，與世界接軌？

學習英文的目的，就是要讓自己在這個資訊爆炸的時代之中，突破語言的藩籬，站在吸收新知的制高點之上，以閱讀獲得力量，以知識創造希望！

針對在英文閱讀中可能面對的挑戰， 我們費心規劃 Reading Power 系列叢書，希望在學習英語的路上助你一臂之力，讓你輕鬆閱讀、快樂學習。

誠摯希望在學習英語的路上， 這套 Reading Power 系列叢書將伴隨你找到閱讀的力量，發揮知識的光芒！

英閱，英悅！

　　從小到大，閱讀對我來說一直是吸收新知、打發時間的最好方法。不管是人物傳記、科學新知或是八卦雜誌，只要有一本書在手，我便不會無聊也自得其樂得很。中文書如此，英文書當然也不例外。因此，英文閱讀於我不僅是英閱，更是英悅！

　　然而，英文閱讀對很多人來說，總好像多了點教科書和考試的味道，少了點與日常生活的連結。所以，雖然讀了很久的英文，但對生活的議題和相關的詞彙用語反而並不那麼熟悉。《英閱百匯》這本書就是從這個理念出發，收集生活中食、衣、住、行、育、樂、環保、品德等各項相關議題而成的一本閱讀書。其中題材從露營到流浪狗，從淨灘到土壤液化，也從如何製作乳酪蛋糕到求職面試；涵蓋很廣，因為生活的面向就是這麼廣！

　　語言的學習，終究要落實在生活中。而這本書就是希望從生活百匯出發帶入閱讀與學習的樂趣，期望能讓英語閱讀成為一件既實用又愉悅的事！

三民 / 東大英語學習教材主編

Contents

Part 4 品德素養

Part 5 商務求職

Part 6 生態保育

Acknowledgements:

The articles in this publication are adapted from the

works by: Michael David Ryan, Peter John Wilds

Photo credits: Depositphotos, 聯合報系提供

Unit 1

Green Island

◆ **Airport:** There are 3 daily flights to Green Island from Taitung. However, the flights are frequently canceled in the winter due to poor weather conditions. Flights must be booked several weeks in advance during the summer months. Planes to and from Green Island seat nineteen passengers and the flight duration is fifteen minutes.

◆ **Green Island Human Rights Cultural Park:** The former jail for political prisoners is now open to visitors. Tourists can visit the museum and exhibition hall to learn about the history.

◆ **Guanyin Cave:** Guanyin Cave was formed by an underground river. There is a stalagmite naturally shaped like Guanyin, Goddess of Mercy, inside the cave. Legend has it that some fishermen were lost at sea but were guided back to shore by a mysterious ball of fire which led them to the Guanyin stalagmite. The fishermen then set up an altar in the cave so that they could worship Guanyin.

◆ **Hiking trail:** There are two short ancient trails on the island. Start your hike from the east side of the island and make your way to the top of Ameishan. The views are spectacular and if you are lucky you may spot a sika deer.

◆ **Zhaori Hot Spring:** Enjoy the sunrise while having a hot spring bath right next to the ocean.

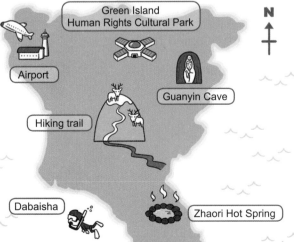

◆ **Dabaisha:** Dabaisha (Big white beach) is a famous diving spot for tourists who want to try snorkeling for the first time as well as for serious scuba divers. It's also a popular location for watching sunsets.

(　　) 1. According to the passage, which of the following is true about the flights to Green Island?

    (A) People can get plane tickets on the spot during summer.

    (B) There are three scheduled flights every day.

    (C) There is one daily flight throughout the summer.

    (D) Flights from Taichung to Green Island are available.

(　　) 2. What is special about Guanyin Cave?

    (A) It is the final resting place of a famous fisherman.

    (B) Sometimes flames come out of the rocks.

    (C) There is a stalagmite shaped like a goddess inside it.

    (D) It is the source of fresh water on the island.

(　　) 3. Which of the following activities is NOT mentioned in the passage?

    (A) Scuba diving.　　　　(B) Hiking.

    (C) Whale watching.　　　(D) Hot spring bathing.

(　　) 4. Where might tourists be able to see a wild deer?

    (A) In the cave.　　　　(B) Near the hot spring area.

    (C) Along the coast.　　　(D) In the center of the island.

(　　) 5. Where would this passage most likely be found?

    (A) In a guidebook.　　　(B) In a library catalog.

    (C) In a medical journal.　　(D) In a press release.

Unit 1

► Vocabulary & Phrases

1. **duration** [djʊ`reʃən] *n.* [U] 持續時間

   * The duration of the speech is 60 minutes.

2. **legend** [`lɛdʒənd] *n.* [C] 傳說

   * Legend has it that a monster lives in the lake.

3. **mysterious** [mɪs`tɪrɪəs] *adj.* 神祕的

   * People are shocked by the mysterious death of the young woman.

4. **worship** [`wɝʃɪp] *vt.* 崇敬，崇拜

   * Believers worship different gods for happiness and blessings.

5. **spectacular** [spɛk`tækjələ] *adj.* 壯觀的，壯麗的

   * People were amazed by the spectacular sunrise over the mountains on the New Year's Day.

6. **location** [lo`keʃən] *n.* [C] 位置

   * The app "Google Map" can show the precise location of the building you are looking for.

7. **catalog** [`kætḷɔg] *n.* [C] 目錄

   * A supermarket catalog can help you find the product you need.

► Words for Recognition

1. Taitung 臺東：位於臺灣本島東南方，面積僅次花蓮縣、南投縣，為臺灣第三大縣。除了自然資源相當豐富外，臺東縣也保留珍貴的原住民文化資產。

2. Guanyin cave 觀音洞：位於綠島東北附近的鐘乳石洞，洞內有座形態似觀世音菩薩的石筍。

3. altar [`ɔltɚ] *n.* [U] 祭壇

4. stalagmite [stə`lægmaɪt] *n.* [C] 石筍

5. Ameishan 阿眉山：位於綠島中心，高 276 公尺，為綠島第二高峰。

6. sika deer 梅花鹿：為臺灣特有亞種。野外族群已在 1969 年左右滅絕。目前墾丁國家公園及綠島的野生族群是由人工復育野放。

7. **Zhaori Hot Spring** 朝日溫泉：經地熱加溫的海水自海岸邊的礁石湧出，形成位於海裡的露天溫泉浴場。

8. **Dabaisha** 大白沙：位於綠島西南端，是綠島最大且最完整的沙灘，也是綠島三大潛水區之一。

9. snorkeling [`snɔrklɪŋ] *n.* [U] 浮潛 (水下呼吸管)

10. scuba diving [`skubə͵daɪvɪŋ] *n.* [U] 水肺潛水 (背氣瓶)

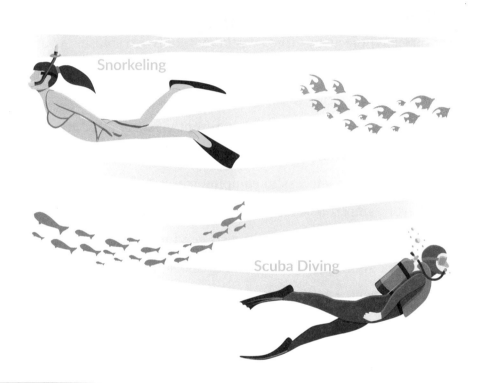

Pop Quiz

_____ 1. The popular singer's private life remains m____s.

_____ 2. The tourists are amazed by the s____r view of the mountains.

_____ 3. L____d has it that the abandoned hospital is haunted by the ghosts.

_____ 4. Some people believe that w____pping gods brings them inner peace.

_____ 5. The shopping mall is in a good l____n which is near the railway station.

Unit 2

Let's Go Camping!

Are you slaving away five weekdays only to waste your precious weekends in front of your TV or computer? You need to get outside. I don't just mean a walk around a neighborhood park. I'm talking about camping!

Camping has become very popular in recent years, and for good reason. It's a great way to experience nature and connect with friends and family. But there's a catch. In order to have a successful camping trip, you have to be well-prepared. If you have never camped before, go with someone who has experience or join a professional organized trip. You will also need a checklist of things to bring. This will include a good-quality tent, hiking shoes, a sleeping bag, bug spray, a raincoat, a warm jacket, a basic first-aid kit, cooking equipment, and sunscreen. And that's just for starters. There are numerous online camping resources that provide a full list of everything you will need. It's also necessary to check the weather conditions before you set off into the wild. For example, if heavy rain is forecast, postponing your trip is the best policy. Finally, always tell a friend or family member when you expect to return from your camping trip.

Going camping can be very enjoyable, but as with any outdoor activity, safety comes first. Camping is a wonderful way to spend your weekend. However, as many people have discovered (including me), it can also be highly addictive! So, if you do get bitten by the camping bug, don't say I haven't warned you!

(　) 1. Which of the following is one of the reasons that the author recommends camping?

(A) It becomes the most popular activity around the world.

(B) It teaches you about wild animals and how to raise them.

(C) It is an activity that everyone must experience once in a lifetime.

(D) It helps you become closer to your friends and family members.

(　) 2. According to the passage, which of the following is what all campers must do?

(A) Go camping with someone who has experience.

(B) Find a neighborhood park suitable for camping.

(C) Prepare well prior to going camping.

(D) Avoid purchasing a second-hand tent.

(　) 3. What should the campers do when heavy rain seems likely?

(A) Join an organized trip.　　　(B) Continue as planned.

(C) Delay their camping trip.　　(D) Inform their family or friends.

(　) 4. What is the tone of this passage?

(A) Encouraging.　　　(B) Pessimistic.

(C) Neutral.　　　(D) Aggressive.

(　) 5. What does the author mean by the last two sentences of the passage?

(A) The author learned his lesson the hard way.

(B) People who once tried camping can't get enough of it.

(C) The author advises others against trying camping alone.

(D) Biting insects are the worst thing about camping.

Vocabulary & Phrases

1. **slave (away)** [slev] *vi.* 拚命工作

   * Lisa has slaved away all day at the report.

2. **There's a catch.** 暗藏玄機。

   * There's a catch, or you couldn't get the house at such a low price.

3. **..., and for good reason.** …是有原因的。

   * Peter is always welcome, and for good reason. He helps others whenever he can.

4. **professional** [prə`fɛʃənḷ] *adj.* 專業的

   * You should listen to the designer's professional opinions.

5. **equipment** [ɪ`kwɪpmənt] *n.* [U] 設備

   * The shop sells various camping equipment.

6. **numerous** [`njumərəs] *adj.* 許多的

   * There are numerous choices of candy in a candy store.

7. **forecast** [`for͵kæst] *vt.* 預報 (forecast, forecast(ed), forecast(ed))

   * The weather reporter forecast(ed) that tomorrow will be a rainy day.

8. **highly** [`haɪlɪ] *adv.* 非常地

   * The United States plays a highly crucial role in the world economy.

9. **pessimistic** [͵pɛsə`mɪstɪk] *adj.* 悲觀的

   * Students are pessimistic about the coming big test.

10. **neutral** [`njutrəl] *adj.* 中立的

    * I always stay neutral when my brothers fight with each other.

11. **aggressive** [ə`grɛsɪv] *adj.* 挑釁的

    * Staring at others is widely regarded as an aggressive behavior.

12. **recommend** [͵rɛkə`mɛnd] *vt.* 推薦，介紹

    * The new hotel is highly recommended for its good service.

13. **prior** [`praɪɚ] *adj.* 事前的，事先的

    * Having prior knowledge of Japanese is one of the requirements for the course.

14. **purchase** [`pɝtʃəs] *vt.* 購買

   *People rushed to purchase basic necessities before the typhoon came.

15. **learn (sth.) the hard way** 吃了苦頭才學會…。

   *The boy had learned a lesson the hard way and he will never hand in his homework late.

Camping checklist 露營清單

1. raincoat 雨衣
2. cooking equipment 烹飪用具
3. hiking shoes 登山鞋
4. basic first-aid kit 基礎急救包
5. sunscreen 防曬乳
6. bug spray 防蟲噴霧
7. warm jacket 保暖外套
8. sleeping bag 睡袋
9. tent 帳篷

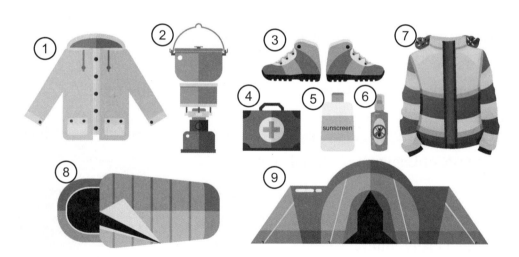

➤ Pop Quiz

_____ 1. In the countryside, you can see n_____s stars at night.

_____ 2. The company p_____ed the land to build a new factory on it.

_____ 3. Many of my friends have r_____ded the new movie to me.

_____ 4. The refugees are p_____c about their future.

_____ 5. Peter is the one who is in charge of office e_____t.

Unit 3

London Rocks!

First stop—Tower Bridge

Built in 1894, the bridge opens up about twice a day to let tall ships pass through. We found out that we had just missed one.

The main event of the day was a sightseeing trip on a red double-decker bus. We really felt like tourists, but that was OK. It was fun and it was a great way to check out the city.

"Take us to see the Queen!"

It turned out she wasn't at home, so we took a photo of Queen's Guards at Windsor Castle.

I want a bearskin!

I've always wanted to ride in a famous black cab in London. And I just took it today. Our driver was really nice and friendly and took us to his favorite fish and chip shop.

French fries are called "chips" in England! Put some salt and vinegar on them. Yummy!

Have the taste of England—Fish and chips!

The dish conquered me with its crispy casing, soft center, and rich flavor. They were so delicious and really filling.

Westminster Abbey

River Thames

Big Ben

Guess where we were! The top of the London Eye! Big Ben, Westminster Abbey and the River Thames are within reach of my sight. What a wonderful way to end our special day in London!

Unit 3

( ) 1. What is this passage mainly about?

    (A) It is a diary written by a local resident.

    (B) It is a dining review written by a reporter.

    (C) It is a travel plan made by a tourist and her friend.

    (D) It is a travel journal kept by a tourist during her trip.

( ) 2. What did the author do at Windsor Castle?

    (A) Took a photo of the guards.

    (B) Participated in a guided tour.

    (C) Went inside to visit the Queen.

    (D) Tried on a bearskin and took a photo.

( ) 3. According to the passage, which of the following statement is true about the black cab in London?

    (A) It may disappear in the near future.

    (B) Drivers lack professional training.

    (C) They are the only way to get around London.

    (D) The author had a great experience of taking one.

( ) 4. How did the author feel when eating fish and chips?

    (A) Dull.   (B) Disgusted.   (C) Enjoyable.   (D) Embarrassed.

( ) 5. Why did the author enjoy the ride on the London Eye?

    (A) It was like a ride on a hot air balloon.

    (B) Famous sights could be seen from the top.

    (C) The Big Ben rang out during her ride on the London Eye.

    (D) The author saw people rowing on the River Thames.

Vocabulary & Phrases

1. **sightseeing** [`saɪt،siɪŋ] *n.* [U] 觀光

   * We will do some sightseeing in Tainan and try the local dishes there.

2. **conquer** [`kɑŋkɚ] *vi. / vt.* 征服

   * The army finally conquered the city.

3. **vinegar** [`vɪnɪgɚ] *n.* [U] 醋

   * You can put some oil and vinegar on your salad.

4. **article** [`ɑrtɪkḷ] *n.* [C] 文章

   * The journalist is writing an article about the super star.

5. **resident** [`rɛzədənt] *n.* [C] 居民

   * Most of the residents here make their living by farming.

6. **disgusted** [dɪs`gʌstɪd] *adj.* 嫌惡的

   * Linda was disgusted at that pile of dirty clothes.

7. **embarrassed** [ɪm`bærəst] *adj.* 尷尬的

   * I felt embarrassed to slip over on the crowded street.

Words for Recognition

1. London 倫敦：英國首都。

2. Tower Bridge 倫敦塔橋：橫跨英國倫敦泰晤士河的高塔式鐵橋。上層為人行道；下層供車輛通過，下層分兩扇橋段，可開啟讓船隻通過。

3. double-decker bus 雙層巴士：雙層公車起源於英國。在倫敦行駛的紅色雙層公車，是受到觀光客歡迎的交通工具。

4. Windsor Castle 溫莎城堡：英國王室的家族城堡。

5. bearskin 黑熊皮高帽：戴上熊皮帽可使士兵看起來更高大。最早由法軍配戴，英軍於滑鐵盧之役擊敗法軍後，便開始戴熊皮帽來顯示自己較法軍強大。

6. England 英格蘭：英國 (大不列顛及北愛爾蘭聯合王國) 其中一個最大的構成國，因此也常代稱英國。

7. the London Eye 倫敦眼：世界上首座最大的觀景摩天輪，目前僅次於中國的南昌之星與新加坡的摩天觀景輪。

8. Big Ben 大笨鐘：坐落泰晤士河畔的西敏寺報時鐘，是倫敦的著名景點。

9. Westminster Abbey 西敏寺：位於倫敦西敏市的哥德式教堂，在 1987 年入列世界文化遺產之一。

10. the River Thames 泰晤士河：位於南英格蘭的河流，對英格蘭許多城市的發展有重大影響，也是倫敦的著名景點。

➤ Pop Quiz

_____ 1. We did some s_____g in Singapore, and took a photo of the famous Merlion statue.

_____ 2. The soldiers c_____red the country's capital at last.

_____ 3. Most people are d_____d at the politician's remarks.

_____ 4. The local r_____ts are looking forward to the construction of the new bridge.

_____ 5. There are growing number of a_____es on diet in magazines.

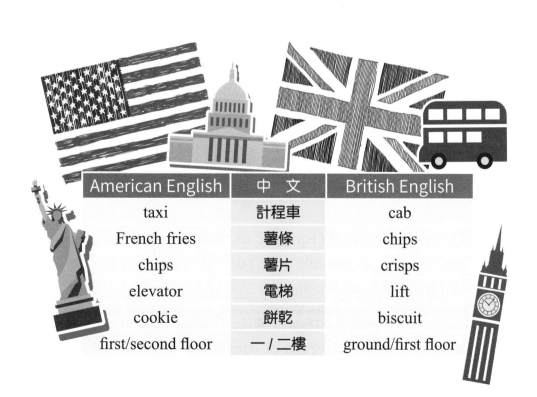

American English	中 文	British English
taxi	計程車	cab
French fries	薯條	chips
chips	薯片	crisps
elevator	電梯	lift
cookie	餅乾	biscuit
first/second floor	一／二樓	ground/first floor

Welcome to Fiji

The Coral Palace Resort: your best choice when visiting Fiji

With nice beachfront views and 5-star hospitality,
here is the perfect place to stay and relax in.

Choose from a range of elegant suites starting from US$ 400 a night, including single / double rooms and 3-bedroom villas, all of which have ocean views. Each room is equipped with a flat-screen TV, free wi-fi, air conditioning, a refrigerator and a private bathroom with a spa. Villas have 1 double bedroom with an en-suite bathroom and 2 single bedrooms. They also feature a large sitting area, a spa bathroom and a fully functional kitchen with a stove, an oven, a microwave and a dishwasher.

We are proud of our 3 award-winning restaurants which can satisfy your dining needs. Each day, you'll have the choice of one of our full buffet, bistro or fine dining restaurants.

✪ For March this year, guests on our suite package will receive a free buffet breakfast each morning.

All our rooms and villas are one minute's walk away from the golden beach where you can enjoy swimming and sunbathing without distraction.

A range of water activities that include snorkeling, scuba diving, surfing lessons, jet skis and beach volleyball are offered.

Our hotel is perfectly equipped to make your vacation as convenient and relaxing as possible with punctual room service, dry cleaning and efficient housekeeping.

Staying in The Coral Palace Resort is an absolute must
if you want to make the most of your Fijian getaway vacation.
For more details, please visit "www.thecoralpalace.com"

(   ) 1. What is the purpose of this passage?

       (A) To promote the hotel.   (B) To review the hotel.

       (C) To hire hotel staff.   (D) To sell the hotel.

(   ) 2. Which of the following is the special offer mentioned in the passage?

       (A) A range of recreational services for all guests.

       (B) Free buffet breakfast for suite package guests.

       (C) Top-quality room service only for villa guests.

       (D) A discount for customers who book villas online.

(   ) 3. Which of the following is NOT one of the features of all the hotel rooms?

       (A) A kitchen.   (B) Free wi-fi.

       (C) Ocean views.   (D) A flat-screen TV.

(   ) 4. According to the passage, where is the hotel most likely located?

       (A) In the mountains.   (B) In the city center.

       (C) Near the ocean.   (D) Next to lake.

(   ) 5. Who would most likely be attracted by this?

       (A) Tourists who love to visit historic sites.

       (B) Tourists who enjoy mountain climbing.

       (C) Tourists who plan to go on a family vacation with a baby.

       (D) Tourists who are especially attracted by water activities.

→ Vocabulary & Phrases

1. **coral** [`kɔrəl] *n.* [U] 珊瑚

   * Due to climate change, coral around the world is dying.

2. **resort** [ˌrɪzɔrt] *n.* [C] 渡假勝地；旅遊勝地

   * All the resorts are crowded with people during weekends.

3. **hospitality** [ˌhɑspɪ`tælətɪ] *n.* [U] 熱情好客；招待

   * The locals show the tourists hospitality with their warm welcome.

4. **elegant** [`ɛləgənt] *adj.* 雅緻的

   * Many couples choose to celebrate Valentine's Day in this elegant restaurant.

5. **villa** [`vɪlə] *n.* [C] 別墅

   * The billionaire has several villas all around the world.

6. **functional** [`fʌŋkʃən!] *adj.* 功能性的

   * A good designer would make his or her designs functional.

7. **distraction** [dɪ`stækʃən] *n.* [U] 心煩意亂，苦惱無聊

   * The loud noise from next class drives me to distraction.

8. **surfing** [`sɝfɪŋ] *n.* [U] 衝浪

   * I used to go surfing on the beach near home every weekend.

9. **equip** [ɪ`kwɪp] *vt.* 裝備；配備

   * All the workers are fully equipped with protective clothing.

10. **punctual** [`pʌŋktʃʊəl] *adj.* 準時的，守時的

    * Most people consider Germans to be fairly punctual.

11. **absolute** [`æbsəˌlut] *adj.* 絕對的；毋庸置疑的

    * The coach has absolute faith in his students; she knows they will win.

12. **make the most of sth.** 充分利用，盡情享受

    * It's the first time my friend and I go travel abroad, so we will definitely make the most of it.

13. **site** [saɪt] *n.* [C] 地點，位置

    * The site of the new restaurant has been decided.

➤ Words for Recognition

1. Fiji 斐濟：位於紐西蘭北方的太平洋島國，擁有美麗的珊瑚礁岸，是著名的
   觀光度假勝地。
2. en-suite [ən-swit] *adj.* (與臥室配套的) 浴室
3. bistro [`bistro] *n.* [C] (尤指法國風格的) 小酒館 (pl. bistros)
4. Fijian [fi`dʒiən] *adj.* 斐濟人；斐濟的
5. getaway [`gɛtə,we] *n.* [C] 假日休閒地

➤ Pop Quiz

_____ 1. Everyone says that Emma is as p____l as a clock for she is never
   late.

_____ 2. The noise of the traffic is driving me to d____n.

_____ 3. Nina is touched by the warm h____y of the homestay family
   because they treat her like their own child.

_____ 4. The company has the a____e confidence in its product.

_____ 5. Rita wears an e____t dress and looks absolutely beautiful.

房型介紹
single room 單人房
twin room 雙床雙人房
double room 一大床雙人房
semi-double room 單床小雙人房
triple room 三人房

Unit 5

Cheese Cake

Everyone loves cheese cake. Unfortunately, delicious and reasonably priced cheese cake is few and far between. Besides, commercial cheese cake usually contains artificial flavor. So, let me show you the cheese cake that is nearly all cream cheese and has crispy crust.

Time:	*Servings:*	*Degree of difficulty:*
7.5 hours	9 inch cake (12 pieces)	Easy

Ingredients

Crust
* 15 digestive biscuits (crushed)
* 2 tablespoons butter (melted)

Filling
* 150 g cream cheese
* 1 ½ cups white sugar
* ¾ cup milk
* 4 eggs
* 1 cup sour cream
* 1 tablespoon natural vanilla extract
* ¼ cup plain flour (sifted)

Steps:

1. Preheat an oven to 170°C. Grease a 9 inch cake pan.

2. Mix crushed digestive biscuits with melted butter. Press the biscuits onto the bottom of the greased cake pan.

3. Mix cream cheese with sugar until smooth. Blend in milk, add the eggs one at a time, and mix them together. Add in sour cream, vanilla extract and flour and then mix all the ingredients until they are finely blended.

4. Pour filling into the prepared cake pan.

5. Bake in the preheated oven for 1 hour. Turn the oven off. Let the cake cool in the oven with the door closed for 5 to 6 hours. (This can prevent the cheese cake from cracking.)

6. Chill the cake in refrigerator before serving it.

Give it a try! Perfect for every occasion.

(   ) 1. What kind of writing is this passage?

      (A) A menu.   (B) A shopping list.

      (C) A recipe.   (D) A dietary guideline.

(   ) 2. Which of the following is NOT one of the ingredients of a cheese cake?

      (A) Eggs.   (B) Sugar.   (C) Butter.   (D) Salt.

(   ) 3. What kinds of cookware are used?

      (A) An oven and a cake pan.

      (B) A frying pan and a cake pan.

      (C) A pot and a measuring cup.

      (D) A frying pan and a measuring cup.

(   ) 4. According to the passage, which of the following statements is true?

      (A) The sugar should be sifted before used.

      (B) The oven needs to be heated in advance.

      (C) It is too hard for beginners to make a cheese cake.

      (D) Baking a cheese cake for 5-6 hours prevents it from cracking.

(   ) 5. Why does the author mean by the last two sentences of the passage?

      (A) To talk readers into being creative.

      (B) To explain why cheese cakes are delicious.

      (C) To emphasize that cheese cakes are expensive.

      (D) To encourage readers to do it at any time at home.

Unit 5

Vocabulary & Phrases

1. **few and far between** 稀少；不常見

   ✻ Recently, jobs are few and far between. It's difficult to find one.

2. **artificial** [ˌɑrtə`fɪʃəl] *adj.* 人工的

   ✻ The artificial flowers are lifelike. At first glance I thought they are real.

3. **crust** [krʌst] *n.* [C][U] 派餅皮

   ✻ The crust is crunchy and full of flavor.

4. **serving** [`sɝvɪŋ] *n.* [C] (食物、飲料等) 一份

   ✻ The recipe is enough for ten servings.

5. **ingredient** [ɪn`gridɪənt] *n.* [C] (烹飪) 材料

   ✻ Bob needs to prepare the ingredients for tomorrow's cooking class.

6. **crush** [krʌʃ] *vt.* 壓碎

   ✻ Crush a handful of nuts and put them into the salad.

7. **grease** [gris] *vt.* 塗油脂於

   ✻ Grease the pan if you want to keep the cake from sticking to the pan.

8. **blend** [blɛnd] *vt.* 使混合

   ✻ Add milk and flour and blend all the ingredients smoothly.

9. **crack** [kræk] *vi. / vt.* 使破裂

   ✻ Hot boiling water makes the glass crack.

10. **recipe** [`rɛsəpɪ] *n.* [C] 食譜

    ✻ This recipe book is for people who have never cooked before.

11. **guideline** [`gaɪdlaɪn] *n.* [C] 指導方針

    ✻ Guidelines prevent people from making mistakes.

12. **talk sb. into sth. / V-ing** 說服⋯去⋯

    ✻ The teacher talks John into studying abroad.

➤ Words for Recognition

1. digestive biscuit [daɪˋdʒɛstɪv] [ˋbɪskɪt] *n.* [C] 消化餅乾

2. tablespoon [ˋtebḷ‚spun] *n.* [C] 一餐匙的量

3. vanilla extract [vəˋnɪlə] [ˋɛkstrækt] *n.* [C][U] 香草精

4. sift [sɪft] *vt.* 過篩

5. dietary [ˋdaɪə‚tɛrɪ] *adj.* 飲食的

➤ Pop Quiz

_____ 1. By following the r_____e, even a beginner can make delicious dishes.

_____ 2. Chance like this is few and far b_____n. You should take it.

_____ 3. C_____hing a large amount of garlic makes my eyes water.

_____ 4. The a_____l leg enables the patient walk.

_____ 5. Some of the windows c_____ked due to the earthquake.

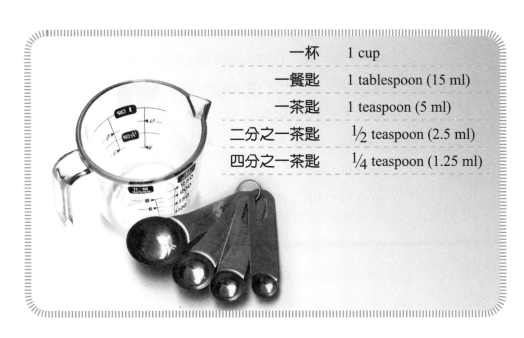

一杯	1 cup
一餐匙	1 tablespoon (15 ml)
一茶匙	1 teaspoon (5 ml)
二分之一茶匙	$\frac{1}{2}$ teaspoon (2.5 ml)
四分之一茶匙	$\frac{1}{4}$ teaspoon (1.25 ml)

Unit 6
Indoor Plants for Your Home or Office

Modern people spend a lot of time indoors and have little contact with nature. For this reason, many people like to have plants in their homes or offices. Research has shown that growing plants indoors can considerably improve the air quality. Not only are certain indoor plants pleasing to look at, but they may also bring other benefits, according to the principles of Chinese feng shui.

The money tree is said to bring good fortune to the person who grows it. Up to five small money trees can be grown in a pot. As the trees grow, they can be patiently twisted together to form a single trunk with an attractive twisting pattern. The money tree is ideal for growing indoors as it prefers low light conditions and only needs to be watered every 7-10 days. If a room is humid, it may produce a nut that you can eat, as well as a flower.

Another indoor plant closely linked with feng shui is recognized as "Lucky Bamboo." It is believed that lucky bamboo can make your home or office peaceful and tranquil. There is a distinctive meaning associated with the number of stalks that the lucky bamboo plant has. For instance, if you are hoping to find a romantic partner, then pick a plant with two stalks. If you are seeking wealth, go for five stalks! And for those wanting good health, grow a plant with seven stalks!

(   ) 1. According to the passage, why do people like to grow plants indoors?

    (A) Because it may be a part of their religious beliefs.

    (B) It's a cheap and convenient entertainment for children.

    (C) There isn't enough space for people to grow plants outdoors.

    (D) They want to bring nature and luck into their homes or offices.

(   ) 2. According to the passage, what is an advantage of growing indoor plants?

    (A) They make the air cleaner.   (B) They match your clothes.

    (C) They can keep bad spirits away.(D) They provide something to talk about.

(   ) 3. What is an interesting way to grow money trees?

    (A) Growing two of them if you are seeking romance.

    (B) Placing them in the dark for up to a week at a time.

    (C) Twisting the trunks of several trees together as they grow.

    (D) Putting five of them in different pots and watch what will happen.

(   ) 4. According to the passage, what advice would you give to someone growing a money tree in their home?

    (A) Keep the leaves wet.   (B) Make sure the air is dry.

    (C) Water it a little every morning. (D) Don't expose it to too much sunlight.

(   ) 5. According to the passage, which of the following would you recommend for someone who wants to be rich?

    (A) Eat the nut grown on a money tree.

    (B) Grow a lucky bamboo plant with five stalks.

    (C) Plant five small money trees in the front garden.

    (D) Place as many plants as possible in the person's home.

Unit 6

➤ Vocabulary & Phrases

1. **research** [`risɜtʃ] *n.* [U] 研究

   ＊Research suggests that exercise is good for health.

2. **up to** 至多

   ＊Up to ten thousand people attended the singing concert.

3. **be said to** 據說

   ＊The man is said to be very rich.

4. **tranquil** [`træŋkwɪl] *adj.* 安寧的

   ＊After retiring, David has led a tranquil life in a small country.

5. **distinctive** [dɪ`stɪŋktɪv] *adj.* 特殊的

   ＊The flower has a very distinctive smell.

6. **associate** [ə`soʃɪˌet] *vt.* 聯想

   ＊The brand is associated with low price and good quality.

7. **stalk** [stɔk] *n.* [C] 莖；柄

   ＊Trimming the flower stalks can make the flower grow better.

8. **entertainment** [ˌɛntɚ`tenmənt] *n.* [C][U] 娛樂

   ＊Hiking is a great family entertainment.

9. **romance** [ro`mæns] *n.* [C] 戀愛

   ＊John and Mary have ended their romance after a huge fight.

10. **expose** [ɪk`spoz] *vt.* 使⋯暴露

    ＊Pregnant women should avoid exposing themselves to secondhand smoke.

Words for Recognition

1. feng shui 風水：堪輿術，指選擇合適的地點的學問。記載選擇宮殿、村落選址、基地建設等方法和原則。

2. money tree 發財樹：原名為馬拉巴栗，原產於墨西哥，是種生命力旺盛、很好栽種的植物。

3. lucky bamboo 富貴竹：原名為辛氏龍血樹，臺灣稱其萬年青，寓意吉祥，是種常見的觀葉植物。

Pop Quiz

_____ 1. The d_____e smell of the fish makes me sick.

_____ 2. What do you usually do for e_____t?

_____ 3. The Chinese a_____e New Year with red envelopes.

_____ 4. The man tried his best to put the r_____e back into his marriage, but failed.

_____ 5. R_____h has proven that smoking is bad for health.

Unit 7
The Netherlands: A Utopia for Bike Riders

To be Dutch is to be a cyclist. Everywhere you go in the Netherlands you can see people riding bicycles. It's a part of everyday life throughout the nation. Bike-sharing systems have grown in popularity in numerous cities worldwide as part of wider efforts to encourage green transportation. However, the Netherlands has embraced the bicycle since long ago and now it has now simply become a part of its culture.

The Netherlands' love affair with the bicycle can be traced back to the Middle East oil crisis in 1973. Urban planners wisely decided to design towns and cities in a way that people could get around easily on bikes. The resulting large network of bicycle paths, bridges and tunnels made the Netherlands a very bicycle-friendly place to live in. Of course, it helps that the Dutch landscape is famously flat. Today, 36% of Dutch people use a bicycle as their main mode of transport on a typical day. There are different types of bike paths in this country. "Bike streets" give priority to bikes, meaning that cars may use them but at speeds below 30 km/h. "Bike-only lanes" often run parallel to the roads and are separated by a barrier, such as a line of trees. "Bicycle highways" are for bicycles only and tend to be used for commuting or exercising. Moreover, there are no traffic lights and **the route** does not cross any regular roads. Bicycle highways are also straight, flat, and especially smooth.

Thanks to the forward-thinking urban planning, traffic rules designed to protect cyclists, and the Dutch people's strong sense of pride in their biking way of life, the Netherlands has become the biking capital of the world. Obviously, the Dutch have a lot to teach the rest of the world about biking.

(   ) 1. What is the first paragraph mainly about?

    (A) The Dutch have built a modern society for a long time.

    (B) Bicycles are the best solution to traffic jams.

    (C) Most people in the Netherlands dislike cars.

    (D) Riding bicycles has long been a part of Dutch culture.

(   ) 2. Which of the following statements about the Netherlands is true?

    (A) There are not a lot of hills or mountains.

    (B) At least 50% of Dutch people own more than two bikes.

    (C) It depends on oil imported from the Middle East.

    (D) Dutch people are forced to ride the bikes.

(   ) 3. What is true about "Bike streets"?

    (A) There are curves on the roads.

    (B) Cars are allowed to drive on them.

    (C) "Bike streets" run parallel to the roads.

    (D) Cyclist must not break the 30 km/h speed limit.

(   ) 4. What does "**the route**" in the second paragraph most likely refer to?

    (A) Bike streets.   (B) Bike-only lanes.

    (C) Bicycle highways.   (D) All of the bike paths.

(   ) 5. Which of the following can be inferred from the passage?

    (A) Other countries can certainly learn from the Netherlands.

    (B) The Netherlands has solved the Middle East oil crisis.

    (C) Too many bicycle paths, bridges, and tunnels make the car drivers in the Netherlands mad.

    (D) People who commute by bike will soon make up 36% of the population in the Netherlands.

Unit 7

➤ Vocabulary & Phrases

1. **popularity** [ˌpɑpjə`lærətɪ] *n.* [U] 受歡迎，流行

   * The increasing popularity of jogging makes the company launch a new line of sporting goods.

2. **transportation** [trænspɚ`teʃən] *n.* [U] 運輸

   * Common green transportation includes walking and biking.

3. **embrace** [ɪm`bres] *vt.* 欣然接受 (意見)

   * A good leader should embrace other's opinions.

4. **urban** [`ɚbən] *adj.* 都市的

   * Many young people move to the urban areas to find a job.

5. **landscape** [`lænskep] *n.* [C] 風景

   * The dramatic landscape attracts millions of tourists every year.

6. **mode** [mod] *n.* [C] 方式

   * Line becomes a popular mode of communication in Taiwan.

7. **priority** [praɪ`ɔrətɪ] *n.* [U] 優先權

   * Drivers should give priority to fire trucks, ambulances or police cars.

8. **parallel** [`pærəˌlɛl] *adj.* 平行的

   * The street trees are parallel to the roads.

9. **barrier** [`bærɪɚ] *n.* [C] 障礙

   * The police restricted the protesters to the area behind the barriers.

10. **commute** [kə`mjut] *vi.* 通勤

    * The student commutes from Keelung to Taipei every day.

11. **moreover** [mor`ovɚ] *adv.* 而且

    * The food there is inexpensive. Moreover, it tastes delicious.

12. **route** [rut] *n.* [C] 路線

    * The cycle route is along the river.

13. **paragraph** [`pærəˌgræf] *n.* [C] 段落

    * The author asks the readers a question in the opening paragraph.

14. **refer to** 談及

　＊Teresa always refers to her pet as her son.

15. **curve** [kɝv] *n.* [C] 彎曲

　＊Drive slowly. This mountain road is full of curves.

16. **infer** [ɪn`fɝ] *vt.* 推論

　＊I can infer Martin's anger from his expression.

➤ Words for Recognition

1. the Netherlands 荷蘭：位於歐洲西部。國名意思為「低窪之國」。境內約有三分之一國土低於海平面。

2. Utopia [ju`topɪə] *n.* [C][U] 烏托邦，完美理想之地

3. Dutch [dʌtʃ] *adj.* 荷蘭的；荷蘭人的；荷蘭語

➤ Pop Quiz

_____ 1. Today is cold, and m____r, it starts snowing.

_____ 2. The pressing project should have p____y over the others.

_____ 3. The mayor wins p____y with the citizens.

_____ 4. The mountains are the natural b____r between the two countries.

_____ 5. A growing number of people e____e the concept of environmental protection.

Unit 8
The Cost of Being a Stay-at-Home Parent

In the 1970s and 1980s, mothers were actively encouraged to pursue their own careers. This gave moms a greater sense of freedom and independence as well as money. Since the 1990s, attitudes toward work-life balance have evolved and now some women feel comfortable about choosing to stay at home to take care of the kids while the father goes out to work. However, taking care of kids and doing the household chores is a much tougher job than most people realize. Besides, they never get a day off and there's no salary at all!

Research shows that if a mother were to receive payment for everything she does in the family, from cooking and driving to cleaning and raising a child, she would need to be paid around US$ 60,000 a year. When you think about what a stay-at-home mom has to do at home, it's clear that she has a job in a very real sense. A family would probably have to spend their entire income just to cover the cost of hiring someone to do all those tasks and chores that a stay-at-home mom does.

Of course, it goes without saying that the job of a stay-at-home parent can be done by a mom or a dad. Thus, no matter which parent has decided to take on **the challenge**, we should all take a moment to express our gratitude for the tough, unpaid work that they do each and every day.

(　　) 1. What is the first paragraph mainly about?

　　(A) Married men refuse to be stay-at-home parents.

　　(B) The media has told women to become stay-at-home parents.

　　(C) Running the household is harder than most people think.

　　(D) Poor working conditions make women choose to stay at home.

(　　) 2. What is the purpose of the second paragraph?

　　(A) The cost of hiring a housemaid is rising.

　　(B) Fathers should take on more responsibility.

　　(C) Stay-at-home parent does a huge amount of work.

　　(D) It's not worthwhile to become a parent and bringing up a family.

(　　) 3. According to the passage, what would happen if people paid others to do all the household chores?

　　(A) The family would receive benefits from the government.

　　(B) The family would need to move into a larger apartment.

　　(C) People should contact a lawyer beforehand before making the decision.

　　(D) The family might need to spend the whole salary to pay the workers.

(　　) 4. What does "**the challenge**" in the last paragraph refer to?

　　(A) Balancing the career and the home life.

　　(B) Looking after the kids and managing the household.

　　(C) Earning enough money to hire a housemaid.

　　(D) Deciding which parent to be the stay-at-home parent.

(　　) 5. What does the author suggest in the last paragraph?

　　(A) Let's show our appreciation to stay-at-home parents.

　　(B) Starting a family is probably a considerable challenge.

　　(C) Both parents need to work these days to support the family.

　　(D) The government should support families with many children.

Vocabulary & Phrases

1. **career** [kə`rɪr] *n.* [C] 職業

   ＊Ariana has decided on a career as a singer since she was five.

2. **evolve** [ɪ`vɑlv] *vi / vt.* 逐漸演變

   ＊If you don't solve the small problem, it could evolve into a big one.

3. **household** [`haʊsˌhold] *n.* [C] 家庭

   ＊It is reported that most of the households in this city own at least a computer.

4. **chore** [tʃor] *n.* [C] 雜務

   ＊The boy will go and play with his friends after he has done the chores.

5. **tough** [tʌf] *adj.* 艱難的

   ＊It is a tough decision for most students to make when it comes to which department to study in.

6. **salary** [`sælərɪ] *n.* [C][U] 薪水

   ＊Linda was on a good salary in her last job.

7. **counsel** [`kaʊnsḷ] *vt.* 建議

   ＊The doctor counsels the patient to stop drinking alcohol.

8. **in a (very) real sense** 事實上 (強調⋯為真)

   ＊Friends influence a person a lot in a very real sense.

9. **go without saying** 不用說；顯而易見

   ＊It goes without saying that the Internet is a two-edged sword.

10. **take a moment** 花一點時間

    ＊It will take a moment to upgrade the computer.

11. **gratitude** [`grætəˌtjud] *n.* [U] 感謝，感激之情

    ＊The movie director expresses her gratitude to the film crew.

12. **beforehand** [bɪ`forˌhænd] *adv.* 預先

    ＊All the food for the party will be prepared beforehand.

13. **appreciation** [əˌpriʃɪ`eʃən] *n.* [U] 感謝

    ＊The students wrote their teacher a card to show their appreciation.

Pop Quiz

_____ 1. We take turns to do the household c_____es.

_____ 2. Peter showed his g_____e to his friends for their help.

_____ 3. The expert c_____ls people not to buy house now.

_____ 4. Over the years, the food stand has e_____ed into a chain restaurant.

_____ 5. After graduating, Athena started her c_____r as a math teacher.

修理傢俱
repair the furniture

上班
go to work

洗衣服
do the laundry

吸地板
vacuum the floor

拖地
mop the floor

準備三餐
prepare the meals

記帳
track the spending

照顧小孩
look after the child

洗碗
do the dishes

燙衣服
iron the clothes

刷浴室
scrub the bathroom

The Cost of Being a Stay-at-Home Parent

Matsu is About to Head Out

Matsu's march is around the corner and it is going to be bigger than ever. It is predicted that over 5 million followers and tourists are going to take part in this huge nine-day event.

The Dajia Matsu Pilgrimage Procession celebrates the birthday of Taiwan's favorite deity, Matsu, the goddess of the sea. Every year on the 23rd day of the 3rd month on the Chinese lunar calendar, worshipers pray, feast and party to celebrate it. The festival is focused on the procession of Matsu's sedan chair as "she" goes from temple to temple inspecting her territory in and around Taichung.

Matsu's statue, along with up to 200,000 pilgrims, starts at the Dajia Jenn Lann Temple in Taichung City and then travels over 300 kilometers through central Taiwan, stopping at more than 100 temples over a nine-day period before returning. At each stop, Matsu is welcomed by fireworks, parades, and performances. It is believed that when Matsu's statue meets other Matsu statues at the temples, she will bring good luck to the temples and people there.

Followers walk for 12 hours each day, carrying Matsu's chair from temple to temple. At each temple, they collect and tie fu (a piece of paper that written with spells) on to their flags to show their commitment to Matsu.

The Matsu pilgrimage is considered by UNESCO to be a world **intangible** asset and it is easy to see why this cultural activity can be one of these assets. For those who wish to experience this magnificent event please visit http://www.dajiamazu.org.tw for more details.

(   ) 1. What is the best title for this passage?

      (A) The Dajia Matsu is Coming to Town

      (B) The Dajia Matsu and the Worshipers

      (C) The Ways of Greeting the Dajia Matsu

      (D) The Dajia Matsu Pilgrimage and Its Origins

(   ) 2. What is the first paragraph mainly about?

      (A) Opinions from faithful believers of Matsu.

      (B) The meaning and origins of the Dajia Matsu.

      (C) The scale of the Dajia Matsu Pilgrimage procession.

      (D) The date and time of the Dajia Matsu Pilgrimage procession.

(   ) 3. According to the passage, which of the following is believed to happen when the Matsu's statue meets other Matsu statues at the temples?

      (A) Other Matsu statues will lead the pilgrimage procession next year.

      (B) The Matsu statues will be tied together for 12 hours.

      (C) Pilgrims and believers should stay away from the temples during that time.

      (D) Good fortune will be brought to the people and temples there.

(   ) 4. According to the passage, why do the followers collect fu?

      (A) It means good luck.

      (B) It means Matsu fail to be there.

      (C) To show how much they worship Matsu.

      (D) Burning the paper symbols can make a fortune.

(   ) 5. What does "**intangible**" in the last paragraph most likely refer to?

      (A) Invisible.   (B) Personal.   (C) Movable.   (D) National.

Unit 9

Vocabulary & Phrases

1. **(just) around the corner** (時間；距離) 很近；在附近

   * The Christmas party is just around the corner.

2. **predict** [prɪ`dɪkt] *vt.* 預測

   * The experts predict that the economy won't recover in ten years.

3. **procession** [prə`sɛʃən] *n.* [C] 隊伍

   * The streets have been closed for the carnival procession.

4. **lunar** [`lunɚ] *adj.* 陰曆的

   * The dragon boat festival is on May 5th of the lunar calendar.

5. **feast** [fist] *vi.* 盡情享用

   * The guests had a great time feasting on steak and wine.

6. **pilgrim** [`pɪlgrɪm] *n.* [C] 朝聖者；進香客

   * Pilgrims are orderly visiting the temple.

7. **commitment** [kə`mɪtmənt] *n.* [U] 奉獻

   * The commitment the volunteers shown is really impressive.

8. **asset** [`æsɛt] *n.* [C] 資產，財產

   * The company sold part of its assets to pay off its debts.

9. **magnificent** [mæg`nɪfəsn̩t] *adj.* 壯觀的；極佳的

   * All the audiences are amazed by the magnificent performance.

10. **faithful** [`feθfəl] *adj.* 忠實的

    * Linda, who never turns her back on me, is truly my faithful friend.

Words for Recognition

1. Matsu 媽祖：宋朝人，本名林默，二十八歲時為救父喪生，而後得道升天，成為中國沿海地區及臺灣人普遍信仰的海上神明。

2. Dajia Matsu Pilgrimage Procession 大甲媽祖進香遶境：臺中大甲鎮瀾宮，於每年農曆三月間舉行長達九天八夜的大甲媽祖出巡遶境活動。

3. deity [`diətɪ] *n.* [C] 女神

4. sedan chair [sɪ`dæn] [tʃɛr] *n.* [C] 轎子

5. Dajia Jenn Lann Temple 大甲鎮瀾宮：位於臺中市大甲區，主奉天上聖母媽祖，為臺灣媽祖信仰的知名廟宇之一。

6. Taichung 臺中：位在臺灣中部，為臺灣人口排名第二的城市。

7. UNESCO (United Nations Educational, Scientific and Cultural Organization) 聯合國教科文組織：宗旨為通過教育、科學及文化來促進各國之間合作，並對和平與安全有所貢獻。

8. fu 符：用以避邪、驅使鬼神的神祕文字。

9. intangible [ɪn`tændʒəbl̩] *adj.* 無形的

▶ Pop Quiz

_____ 1. The palace is a m____t building which attracts many visitors.

_____ 2. The exam is around the c____r. You'd better start to study.

_____ 3. That company owns many foreign a____ts such as factories in China and India.

_____ 4. Bob has been a f____l member of the church for years.

_____ 5. The typhoon is p____ted to hit the island tonight.

Unit 10
Estonia's Young Coders

We are living in an age of information technology. Complex systems lie at the heart of many aspects of our daily lives, from our electricity supply to our smartphones. The language that enables these vital systems to function is known as computer code. Writing computer code is considered such an important skill that it is now being taught to a new generation of coders in Europe, the United States and many other countries around the world. Some countries, such as China and Estonia, are even teaching kids as young as seven to code.

Estonia made the headlines when it first introduced a nationwide coding education program to children ranging from 7 to 19. When these technologically literate students graduate and enter the job market, it's hoped that their coding skills will give them a great advantage. As new technologies emerge, Estonia will be able to receive the benefits of having a workforce with a strong background in coding. A number of European countries — France, Spain, Slovakia, England, and Finland—were quick to follow Estonia's lead and had already added coding into their national primary school curricula. In addition to having the skills needed for coding, children will learn logical thinking and problem-solving skills, which can be applied beyond the field of information technology.

Coding is an international language that is only going to grow in importance. It's hard to predict what the future holds. However, it does seem clear that in the coming decades, countries that neglect to teach their citizens coding from a young age could very well be left behind in the global economy.

(   ) 1. What is the author's attitude toward the coding education program in Estonia?

(A) Defensive.   (B) Negative.   (C) Supportive.   (D) Indifferent.

(   ) 2. According to this passage, why is it necessary to teach kids to code?

(A) It is fun and interesting.

(B) It is an increasingly important skill.

(C) It prevents kids from playing games.

(D) It helps kids learn foreign languages.

(   ) 3. Why did Estonia make the headlines?

(A) It has the best coders in the world.

(B) It began teaching young kids how to code.

(C) Its economy was saved by its young coders.

(D) It allowed kids to go to college to learn coding.

(   ) 4. Aside from coding, what else do primary school kids in Europe need to learn?

(A) How to think logically.

(B) How to become a leader.

(C) How to make a computer.

(D) How to develop their people skills.

(   ) 5. Which of the following can be inferred from the final paragraph?

(A) International education is a growing business.

(B) Learning to code might actually be a complete waste of time.

(C) If countries don't teach kids to code, their economy may suffer.

(D) Countries must increase their production of technology products.

▶ Vocabulary & Phrases

1. **information** [ˌɪnfəˈmeʃən] *n.* [U] 資訊，情報；知識

   ＊Nowadays, people usually use the Internet to collect information.

2. **aspect** [ˈæspɛkt] *n.* [C] 觀點；角度

   ＊Climate is an important aspect of farming.

3. **vital** [ˈvaɪtl̩] *adj.* 不可或缺的

   ＊Creativity is vital to the success of a company.

4. **code** [kod] *n.* [C][U] 電腦的程式碼｜*vt.* 編碼

   ＊Learning code is important for finding jobs.

   ＊Coding is actually not that difficult as I thought.

5. **generation** [ˌdʒɛnəˈreʃən] *n.* [C] 世代

   ＊People of the younger generation have grown up without the experience of using videotape.

6. **technologically** [ˌtɛknəˈladʒɪkl̩ɪ] *adv.* 科技地

   ＊Germany is one of the technologically advanced countries in Europe.

7. **literate** [ˈlɪtərɪt] *adj.* 會讀寫的

   ＊Being literate is not easy in ancient times; most people could not read.

8. **emerge** [ɪˈmɝdʒ] *vi.* 嶄露頭角

   ＊Some new technology companies have emerged recently.

9. **curriculum** [kəˈrɪkjələm] *n.* [C] 課程 (pl. curricula, curriculums)

   ＊Math is a necessary part of the school curriculum.

10. **logical** [ˈladʒɪkl̩] *adj.* 合理的，合乎邏輯的

    ＊It is a logical conclusion that the man is the murderer.

11. **neglect** [nɪˈglɛkt] *vt.* 忽視

    ＊Neglecting minor problems might cause a great disaster.

12. **economy** [ɪˈkanəmɪ] *n.* [C] 經濟

    ＊The world economy has been growing in recent years.

13. **defensive** [dɪˈfɛnsɪv] *adj.* 戒備的

    ＊Unhappy childhood made Julia a defensive person.

人文科學

14. **indifferent** [ɪnˋdɪfrənt] *adj.* 漠不關心的

＊The company is criticized for being indifferent to labor rights.

15. **production** [prəˋdʌkʃən] *n.* [U] 產量

＊The power went off unexpectedly, so there was a huge decline in production.

➡ Words for Recognition

1. workforce [ˋwɝkˏfors] *n.* [C] 勞動力
2. supportive [səˋportɪv] *adj.* 支持的

➡ Pop Quiz

_____ 1. The p____n has doubled since using the new machine.

_____ 2. Thanks to the education policy, most of the people are l____e now.

_____ 3. A war could damage a region's e____y seriously.

_____ 4. The government should examine the new policy from every a____t to predict its effect.

_____ 5. Water is v____l for one's health.

Unit 11

Swim Safe This Summer

Attention all parents:

As you may know, summer vacation is fast approaching and we are sure that involves many water-based activities and outings. This is just a friendly reminder about water safety to help keep your children safe this summer.

The most important thing is to make sure your children understand their own swimming ability so that they can make proper decisions when in the water.

Swimming in the ocean comes with a great many challenges you won't face in the swimming pool. The sea will always require more effort to swim in, so make sure the children know that they won't be able to do the same things in the sea as they can in the pool. Also, natural currents tend to move people in a certain direction. Children have to be aware of where they are relative to the shore. The safest area of the water will be the one between the flags placed by the lifeguards. Children must never swim beyond the area.

While the swimming pool is generally a more controlled environment, it comes with its own unique dangers. Slipping around the pool area is the most common problem. That's why your children should walk whenever they are out of the pool. Moreover, they can only dive in the designated area to avoid both hitting the pool floor and colliding with other swimmers.

For more information about water safety, you can read online at www.swimsafe.gov/childsafety

Thank you,
Albany Primary School

( ) 1. What is the purpose of this passage?

(A) To remind students to be aware of water safety during summer vacation.

(B) To inform parents of water safety due to the upcoming summer vacation.

(C) To prepare for an outing that the school is planning for the upcoming holidays.

(D) To give tips for teachers and students to prevent them from drowning in the swimming pool.

( ) 2. According to the passage, which of the following statements is true about swimming in the ocean and pools?

(A) Pools are more dangerous.   (B) The ocean is more dangerous.

(C) They are equally safe.   (D) They are equally dangerous.

( ) 3. Which of the following was specifically mentioned in the passage that children need to pay attention when swimming in the ocean?

(A) Whether a shark is nearby.

(B) Whether there is a safeguard.

(C) The length of time they stay in the ocean.

(D) Their locations in relation to the shore.

( ) 4. Why should children only dive in the designated area in a swimming pool?

(A) To keep them in line.

(B) To keep them from slipping.

(C) To prevent them from hitting the pool floor.

(D) To keep them from splashing water everywhere.

(   ) 5. Which of the following is true about this passage?

    (A) It is a letter sent by a primary school.

    (B) It is a letter to teach children how to swim.

    (C) Personal information can be found in the letter.

    (D) It should be signed by the parents and sent back to the school.

➤ Vocabulary & Phrases

1. **involve** [ɪnˋvɑlv] *vt.* 包含

    ＊ The job involved going on business trips to other countries.

2. **outing** [ˋaʊtɪŋ] *n.* [C] 出遊

    ＊ The students will go on a class outing to the amusement park.

3. **reminder** [rɪˋmaɪndɚ] *n.* [C] 提醒 (的事物)

    ＊ I wrote myself a reminder to take out the trash.

4. **a great many** 很多

    ＊ There are a great many candies prepared for Halloween.

5. **relative** [ˋrɛlətɪv] *adj.* 相對的

    ＊ The position of the moon relative to the earth changes every day.

6. **unique** [juˋnik] *adj.* 獨特的，特有的

    ＊ Some foreign tourist can't stand the unique smell of stinky tofu.

7. **designate** [ˋdɛzɪɡˏnet] *vt.* 指定，劃定

    ＊ This area of the station has been designated for smokers.

8. **collide** [kəˋlaɪd] *vi.* 相撞

    ＊ As the boy fell, his head collided with the stairs.

9. **safeguard** [ˋsefˏɡɑrd] *n.* [C] 保護措施

    ＊ People purchase insurance as a safeguard against any unexpected accident.

Pop Quiz

_____ 1. It is a u_____e experience for me to live in the desert.

_____ 2. The fight i_____ed teenagers, adults and police.

_____ 3. This area is d_____ed as a parking lot.

_____ 4. The two cars c_____ed with each other.

_____ 5. Children are looking forward to the family o_____g.

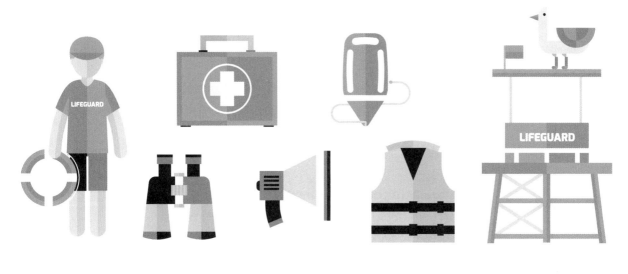

Unit 12

A Common LINE Scam

Below are the excerpts from Dave's text messages.

Aug 19 (Sat)

Fraud

Here's a friendly reminder about a common scam on LINE. Always be suspicious if a LINE friend asks you for money. It is almost certainly a scam if your LINE friend asks you to enter a 4-digit code. It means that someone probably has taken over your friend's LINE account. If you enter the code, you are actually allowing this person to take over your LINE account as well. Call our fraud hotline at 165 if you have any questions.

12:30 PM

◀ Amy

Aug 20 (Sun)

Amy

Hey Dave! I'm in a bit of trouble at the moment. I need a favor.

1:00 PM

Read
1:05 PM **What's going on?**

Amy

I'm actually in the hospital now. I was in a motorcycle accident. It's not serious, but I need some money to pay the hospital bill.

1:05 PM

Read
1:05 PM **That should be covered by National Health Insurance.**

Amy

Right. Unfortunately, I've lost my health card so until that's sorted out I need to pay in cash. I can get the money back once I've done all the paperwork.

1:08 PM

Read
1:10 PM **How much do you need?**

Amy

NT$28,500. Can you help me out? Please! My bank account number is 904-306-12001. You'll receive a text message from my bank asking you to confirm your phone number. Just enter the 4-digit code. I'll pay you back next week, I promise.

1:18 PM

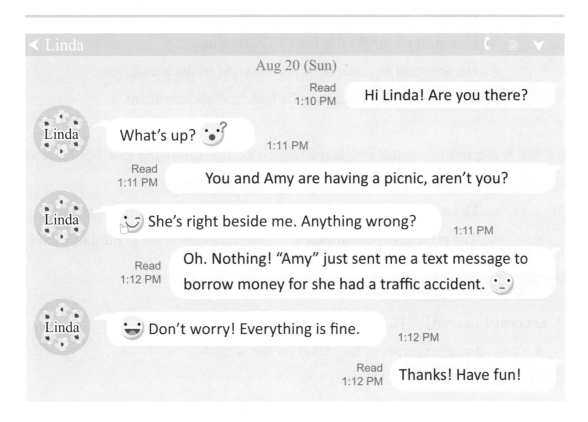

Linda

Aug 20 (Sun)

Read 1:10 PM — Hi Linda! Are you there?

Linda — What's up? 1:11 PM

Read 1:11 PM — You and Amy are having a picnic, aren't you?

Linda — She's right beside me. Anything wrong? 1:11 PM

Read 1:12 PM — Oh. Nothing! "Amy" just sent me a text message to borrow money for she had a traffic accident.

Linda — Don't worry! Everything is fine. 1:12 PM

Read 1:12 PM — Thanks! Have fun!

(   ) 1. Which of the following best describes Dave's action?

    (A) Alert.   (B) Devoted.   (C) Foolish.   (D) Encouraging.

(   ) 2. What does the anti-fraud message warn about?

    (A) Sharing personal information with LINE friends.

    (B) Calling the police hotline for more information.

    (C) Entering a 4-digit code at a friend's request for financial aid.

    (D) Sending personal details to LINE users whom you have never met in person.

(   ) 3. According to the messages, why did Amy ask Dave for money?

    (A) To pay a parking fine.   (B) To get her motorcycle fixed.

    (C) To pay her medical bill.   (D) To buy food for the picnic.

Unit 12

(   ) 4. What might be the reason why Dave didn't agree to Amy's request?

        (A) He didn't have enough cash on hand.

        (B) He could no longer use his LINE account.

        (C) He was mad because he wasn't invited to the picnic.

        (D) He remembered a warning he had read about a scam.

(   ) 5. According to the messages, which of the following can be inferred about Amy's LINE account?

        (A) Dave had deleted it.   (B) A scammer had taken it over.

        (C) The police had controlled it.   (D) It was under the control of Linda.

▶ Vocabulary & Phrases

1. **excerpt** [`ɛksɝpt] *n.* [C] 摘錄

   ＊You can read excerpts of the novel on the website.

2. **fraud** [frɔd] *n.* [C][U] 詐騙 (罪)

   ＊There are increasing victims of the credit card fraud.

3. **suspicious** [sə`spɪʃəs] *adj.* 懷疑的；可疑的

   ＊The man's behavior is very suspicious; we need to keep an eye on him.

4. **at the moment** 此刻，目前

   ＊The woman is sad and wants to be left alone at the moment.

5. **insurance** [ɪn`ʃʊrəns] *n.* [U] 保險

   ＊I always buy insurance before traveling abroad.

6. **help sb. out** 幫助…擺脫 (困境)

   ＊Michelle helped her partner out by spending time with her.

7. **alert** [ə`lɝt] *adj.* 警覺的

   ＊The dog is alert to strangers.

8. **devoted** [dɪ`votɪd] *adj.* 摯愛的

   ＊Lily is devoted to all kinds of animals and wants to be a vet.

9. **financial** [faɪ`nænʃəl] *adj.* 財務的；金融的

   ＊The company has faced financial difficulty.

生活百科

Words for Recognition

1. scam [`skæm] *n.* [C] 詐欺

   scammer [`skæmɚ] *n.* [C] 詐欺犯
2. digit [`dɪdʒɪt] *n.* [C] 數字
3. delete [dɪ`lit] *vi. / vt.* 刪除

Pop Quiz

_____ 1. Just in case, I have bought car i_____e.

_____ 2. The country is facing f_____l crisis now and needs foreign aid.

_____ 3. The man's behavior was s_____s, so the police officer went forward and asked him questions.

_____ 4. Sorry, the manager is in a meeting at the m_____t, so she can't come to the phone now.

_____ 5. The small animal is always a_____t to the dangers.

Unit 13

Tracy's Schedule for February

SUN	MON	TUE
2/1	2/2	2/3
2/8	2/9 10:00 New advertising campaign for Zed Battery 14:00 Brainstorming session for Klara Shampoo TV ad	2/10 13:30 Advertising conference: Network like crazy!
2/15 Sunrise! Sightseeing around Melbourne! Fly back to Taoyuan. Flight departs at 20:15	2/16 DAY OFF	2/17 19:00 Dinner with Dave at Papa Manos
2/22 Camping on Green Island with Dave	2/23	2/24 11:00 Interview with Media Talk, Top FM. First time on a national radio! Don't Be Nervous!

( ) 1. Which of the following has Tracy scheduled in the first week of February?

(A) A job interview.   (B) A trip to the veterinarian.

(C) A dinner party.   (D) A date with her boyfriend.

( ) 2. Which of the following does Tracy intend to spend time doing in Melbourne?

(A) Creating new advertisements.

(B) Promoting her clients' products.

(C) Hiring new employees for her company.

(D) Finding new customers at the exposition.

WED	THU	FRI	SAT
2/4 09:30 Meeting with a new client — OK Cola	*2/5* 08:30-12:00 First training session for new employees	*2/6* Take Mocha to the vet. Meow!	*2/7* 07:00 Go hiking with Mary on the Sandiaoling Trail.
2/11 Fly to Melbourne. Flight departs at 23:00 Ugh!	*2/12* 19:00 Have dinner with the sales manager of KiWi, Amber New Prospect!	*2/13* 14:30 Meeting with a new client — Kangaroo Cookies	*2/14* 10:00 Attend the Advertising Expo. Find new customers! Get an early night. (21:00 at the latest!!!)
2/18 09:00 Monthly budget meeting	*2/19* 08:30-12:00 Hold first round of interviews for a new art director.	*2/20* 20:00 Retirement party for sales director, Bill, at Pippa's Bar	*2/21* Camping on Green Island with Dave
2/25 21:30 Video conference call with the New York office	*2/26*	*2/27* 19:00 An appointment at the dentist's	*2/28* Happy birthday to me! Movie and dinner with Dave

(   ) 3. According to the passage, which of the following statements is true?

(A) Tracy raises a puppy called Mocha.

(B) Tracy will stay in Melbourne for five days.

(C) One of Tracy's colleagues will retire in February.

(D) Tracy will go hiking with her pet on Feb. 7th.

Tracy's Schedule for February

Unit 13

(   ) 4. What is going to happen on February 24th?

      (A) Tracy will be on a national radio program.

      (B) Tracy will become a radio DJ for the morning.

      (C) Tracy will negotiate with a media company.

      (D) Tracy will be interviewed for a new job.

(   ) 5. According to the passage, which place does Tracy most likely live in?

      (A) Melbourne.   (B) Taipei.   (C) Green Island. (D) New York.

➤ Vocabulary & Phrases

1. **session** [ˈsɛʃən] *n.* [C] (活動、會議的) 一段時間

  ＊The government has provided training sessions for the unemployed.

2. **veterinarian** [ˌvɛtrəˈnɛrɪən] *n.* [C] 獸醫 (亦作 vet)

  ＊The dog hit by a car should be taken to a veterinarian as soon as possible.

3. **campaign** [kæmˈpen] *n.* [C] 活動

  ＊The company has organized the advertising campaign for three months.

4. **battery** [ˈbætərɪ] *n.* [C] 電池

  ＊The battery is flat. You can find a new one in the drawer.

5. **conference** [ˈkɑnfərəns] *n.* [C] 會議

  ＊There would be several conferences on information security.

6. **depart** [dɪˈpɑrt] *vi. / vt.* 出發

  ＊Flights to Vancouver depart from Terminal 2.

7. **prospect** [ˈprɑspɛkt] *n.* [C][U] 機會，可能

  ＊There is every prospect that the war will be over after the negotiation.

8. **monthly** [ˈmʌnθlɪ] *adj.* 每月一次的

  ＊Most of the workers get a monthly salary.

9. **retire** [rɪˈtaɪr] *vi. / vt.* 退休

  ＊My grandfather retired at 65.

  retirement [rɪˈtaɪrmənt] *n.* [C][U] 退休

  ＊Experts predict that the retirement age will rise due to population aging.

10. **appointment** [əˋpɔɪntmənt] *n.* [C] 預約

＊Joe has an appointment with a client.

11. **intend** [ɪnˋtɛnd] *vi.* / *vt.* 打算，計劃

＊What do you intend to do after graduation?

12. **colleague** [ˋkɑlig] *n.* [C] 同事

＊This is Cathy Lin, a new colleague in my office.

13. **negotiate** [nɪˋgoʃɪ͵et] *vi.* / *vt.* 談判；協商

＊The US government said they won't negotiate with terrorists.

▶ Words for Recognition

1. Melbourne 墨爾本：位於澳洲東岸維多利亞州南部，是澳洲第二大城市，也被公認是最適宜居住的城市之一。

2. exposition [͵ɛkspəˋzɪʃən] *n.* [C] 博覽會 (亦作 expo)

3. brainstorming [ˋbren͵stɔrmɪŋ] *n.* [U] 自由討論，腦力激盪

4. Taoyuan 桃園：位於臺灣西北部，擁有臺灣規模最大的國際機場。桃園具有閩南、客家、原住民、東南亞新住民等多元族群，孕育了多元的文化資產。

5. New York 紐約：位於美國東北紐約州，是個對全球的經濟、商業、金融、媒體、政治、教育和娛樂具有極大影響力的國際大都會。

6. Sandiaoling 三貂嶺：位在新北市瑞芳區，有著名的三貂嶺古道，沿途風光清幽秀麗，是許多喜歡尋幽訪古的山友的健行路線之一。

7. DJ (Disc Jockey) 唱片騎師：挑選並播放事先錄製的音樂，且於現場以電腦進行混音創作的表演者。

▶ Pop Quiz

_____ 1. The company refused to n_____e with the protesters.

_____ 2. Mary i_____ds to study abroad after graduating from university.

_____ 3. The organization launched a c_____n against bullying.

_____ 4. Did you make an a_____t with your dentist for next month?

_____ 5. The plane d_____ts at 5 A.M. We had better arrive at the airport before 3 A.M.

Greetings from New Zealand

Hey Dave,

I have been here on holiday for less than a week and it has been fantastic so far. New Zealand is a beautiful country.

I have been staying in Queenstown for the last couple of days and I'll never forget it. The landscape here is amazing with the deep bright blue lakes surrounded by snow-capped mountains.

Yesterday I rode on the Shotover Jet, which is a speed boat that goes up and down Gorge River. It was very intense. It went so fast that I could barely keep my eyes open due to the wind and water hitting my face. The driver would often spin the boat splashing icy cold water everywhere, making everyone in the boat wet.

A few days ago, I went to an old Maori settlement which was colonized by Europeans. It was very interesting to see how they lived then. They were strong warriors that hunted large flightless birds called "moa" for food, and almost ate them all. Unfortunately, these birds are now extinct though. Also, I bought some **exquisite** Maori jade carvings at the souvenir shop there.

Tomorrow, I'm going to fly to Auckland in the North Island. It is the biggest city in New Zealand. I have heard Sky Tower is a good place to visit. Apparently it is over 300 meters tall and offers great views of the city. Visitors can also go bungee jumping and enjoy the excitement of jumping off the building. I really like to give it a try.

I'll be back home in a few weeks. See you then.

All the best,

Rob

(   ) 1. Why does Rob describe Queenstown as an unforgettable place?

       (A) He got the chance to meet the queen.

       (B) He went swimming in the bright blue lake.

       (C) He saw the town was capped with snow.

       (D) He thought that the landscape there is extraordinary.

(   ) 2. Which of the following best describes the experience of the Shotover Jet ride?

       (A) Boring.   (B) Peaceful.   (C) Exciting.   (D) Relaxing.

(   ) 3. Which of the following statements is true about moa?

       (A) Maori didn't hunt them for food.

       (B) Moa is a kind of bird that can't fly.

       (C) We still can find them in New Zealand.

       (D) Moa is the national bird of New Zealand.

(   ) 4. What does the word "**exquisite**" in the fourth paragraph most likely mean?

       (A) Delicate.   (B) Delicious.   (C) Shady.   (D) Shallow.

(   ) 5. According to the letter, what might Rob most likely do next after he sent the letter?

       (A) Buy jade carvings.   (B) Fly back home.

       (C) Visit a museum.   (D) Dive off a tall building.

Unit 14

➤ Vocabulary & Phrases

1. **fantastic** [fæn`tæstɪk] *adj.* 極好的

   ＊The weather today is fantastic. We can surely enjoy the picnic.

2. **gorge** [gɔrdʒ] *n.* [C] 峽谷

   ＊Taroko Gorge is a famous tourist attraction in Taiwan.

3. **intense** [ɪn`tɛns] *adj.* 激烈的

   ＊The basketball game became intense in the last 3 minutes.

4. **warrior** [`wɔrɪɚ] *n.* [C] 戰士，勇士

   ＊A noble warrior would not kill innocent people.

5. **extinct** [ɪk`stɪŋkt] *adj.* 絕種的

   ＊We should protect the environment or some endangered species will become extinct.

6. **exquisite** [`ɛkskwɪzɪt] *adj.* 精緻的

   ＊It is the most exquisite painting that I've ever seen.

7. **jade** [dʒed] *n.* [U] 玉

   ＊The woman wears a necklace made of jade.

8. **souvenir** [ˌsuvə`nɪr] *n.* [C] 紀念品

   ＊I bought a bottle of maple syrup as a souvenir of Canada.

9. **extraordinary** [ɪk`strɔrdn̩ˌɛrɪ] *adj.* 不平凡的

   ＊Nightingale who established the principles of nursing is truly an extraordinary woman.

10. **delicate** [`dɛləkət] *adj.* 精緻的

    ＊That delicate jade from Qing dynasty is worth a fortune.

Auckland

→ Words for Recognition

1. New Zealand 紐西蘭：位於太平洋西南部島國，主要由北島和南島組成，地形多變，孕育多樣特有種生物。其風景優美，氣候宜人，旅遊勝地遍布。

2. Queenstown 皇后鎮：位於紐西蘭南島的旅遊渡假勝地。整座城市環繞瓦卡蒂普湖的弗蘭克敦灣建造。群山連綿，湖光山色宛如仙境。

3. Shotover Jet 噴射快艇：於皇后鎮肖托弗河上進行的水上娛樂活動。

4. Maori [`mɑʊri] n. [C] 毛利人 | adj. 毛利的

5. European [ˌjʊrə`piən] n. [C] 歐洲人

6. colonize [`kɑləˌnaɪz] vt. 將⋯建為殖民地

7. moa [`moə] n. [C] 摩亞鳥 (恐鳥)

8. carving [`kɑrvɪŋ] n. [C] 雕刻品

9. Auckland 奧克蘭：紐西蘭北島最大的城市。約有 32％的人居住此城，是紐西蘭工業和商業中心。

10. bungee jumping [`bʌndʒi] [`dʒʌmpɪŋ] n. [U] 高空彈跳

→ Pop Quiz

_____ 1. I love the d_____ e design of the earrings.

_____ 2. J_____ e jewelry is popular among Asians.

_____ 3. Dinosaurs have been e_____ t for a long time.

_____ 4. The man is regarded as a great w_____ r of his tribe.

_____ 5. The scientist's performance was f_____ c and won him a medal.

Sky Tower

Unit 15
The Invisible Hand of Facebook's Algorithms

There are currently 1.86 billion monthly active Facebook users. It's a remarkable number, but an even more amazing fact is that most users read their news feed at least once a day. Facebook uses various **algorithms** to determine what posts appear in a user's news feed. Given the enormous power that Facebook has over many aspects of our lives, these **algorithms** have become a source of much controversy.

Facebook's own research has shown that changing the news feed algorithms can make people happier or sadder. It can also influence users' opinions on various issues. In addition, Facebook is under pressure to deal with the growing problem of fake news on its website. As a result, the way that Facebook manages its algorithms has been a subject of considerable attention in the media. Of course, as a business, Facebook's main goal is to make money. Its algorithms are designed to encourage users to stay on the website for as long as possible so that it can make money by providing targeted advertisements. In this respect, it has been doing a good job so far. In one year alone, Facebook can make $10 billion. However, its algorithms are creepy for they record what the users have read on the Internet. Understandably, Facebook is keen to emphasize that its algorithms can also be a force for good. Its recently implemented suicide prevention algorithms, for instance, could save many lives.

Facebook's algorithms have a huge impact on one-fifth of the world's adult population. Although the **social media giant** certainly provides us with many benefits, it is important to recognize the extent to which people are being influenced by some very clever pieces of code without their knowing.

(   ) 1. What can be inferred from the first paragraph?

    (A) Facebook is becoming less popular.

    (B) Some algorithms could be considered illegal.

    (C) The posts in Facebook users' news feed are selected.

    (D) Many Facebook users have an account but never use it.

(   ) 2. What does the word "**algorithms**" in the first paragraph mean?

    (A) A set of mathematical rules.   (B) A series of instruction books.

    (C) Technical machines.   (D) Customer service principles.

(   ) 3. According to the passage, which of the following might cause the users to quit Facebook?

    (A) A new social networking site comes along.

    (B) The users think Facebook tracks their Internet usage.

    (C) There are too many advertisements on the news feed.

    (D) The users believe that Facebook only cares about money.

(   ) 4. Which of the following positive effects of algorithms does Facebook claim?

    (A) To help users make new friends.

    (B) To examine the quality of online news.

    (C) To reduce the number of advertisements.

    (D) To prevent people from committing suicide.

(   ) 5. What does the phrase "**social media giant**" in the last paragraph refer to?

    (A) Publishers.   (B) Facebook.

    (C) Fake news.   (D) News media.

Unit 15

Vocabulary & Phrases

1. **remarkable** [rɪ`mɑrkəbl̩] *adj.* 顯著的

   ∗ It is remarkable that all the passengers in the accident are safe and sound.

2. **enormous** [ɪ`nɔrməs] *adj.* 巨大的

   ∗ The man earns an enormous amount of money, so he is a billionaire now.

3. **controversy** [`kɑntrə‚vɝsɪ] *n.* [C][U] 爭議

   ∗ The controversy over wearing uniform has existed for many years.

4. **issue** [`ɪʃʊ] *n.* [C] 議題

   ∗ The government has recently been discussing environmental issues.

5. **website** [`wɛb‚saɪt] *n.* [C] 網站

   ∗ You can find more information on the website of the university.

6. **Internet** [`ɪntɚ‚nɛt] *n. sing.* 網際網路

   ∗ People should be aware of the information on the Internet.

7. **understandably** [‚ʌndɚ`stændəblɪ] *adv.* 可以理解地

   ∗ The players were understandably upset about losing their last game.

8. **keen** [kin] *adj.* 熱切的

   ∗ All the fans are keen to shake hands with the pop singer.

9. **implement** [`ɪmplə‚mɛnt] *vt.* 實施 (計畫)

   ∗ The plan is ideal but difficult to implement.

10. **prevention** [prɪ`vɛnʃən] *n.* [U] 預防

    ∗ One of the important functions of education is the prevention of crimes.

11. **impact** [`ɪmpækt] *n.* [C][U] 衝擊

    ∗ The parent's death made huge impact on this little boy.

12. **extent** [ɪk`stɛnt] *n.* [U] 程度

    ∗ The full extent of the flood damage is far beyond our imagination.

13. **series** [`sɪriz] *n.* [C] 一系列

    ∗ The movie series was a huge success at the box office.

14. **publisher** [`pʌblɪʃɚ] *n.* [C] 出版商

    ∗ The writer is looking for a publisher for her novel.

➤ Words for Recognition

1. algorithm [ˋælgəˌrɪðəm] *n.* [C] (電腦) 演算法

➤ Pop Quiz

_____ 1. The next tax policy aroused much c_____y among the citizens.

_____ 2. The actor is k_____n to be chosen as the main character.

_____ 3. The invention is a r_____e achievement for it saves many people's life.

_____ 4. An e_____s amount of people gathered to see the popular singer.

_____ 5. The huge earthquake made a serious i_____t on the locals.

Anti-bullying Poster

STOP BULLYING–SAY SOMETHING

**Take a look at these two children. The one on the left is a bully.
Surprised? Don't be.**

What will bullies do?

The thing about bullies is they often don't actually look like bullies!

But one thing all bullies have in common is that they choose a victim and enjoy being cruel to him or her. Bullies may beat someone, or write mean comments or spread nasty rumors about other classmates online. Most important of all, bullies force others to also be mean to their victims.

How do we stop bullying?

Well, this is where you can come in. Yes, YOU, the person reading this poster. If you know someone is being bullied, then say something.

Tell a trustworthy adult in your school about it. If you think it's better to stay quiet and say nothing, then you may become the next victim.

Let's work together!

Imagine you were the one being bullied. Wouldn't you want someone to help you put an end to your nightmare? Bullies never stop until someone steps forward and says "Enough is enough." Do the right thing and help put a stop to bullying.

(   ) 1. What is the main idea of the poster?

      (A) It is easy to identify a bully.

      (B) Ways to stop bullying behavior.

      (C) All bullies should receive punishment.

      (D) A bully knows when to say enough is enough.

(   ) 2. What do bullies have in common?

      (A) They choose a victim.

      (B) They have nightmares.

      (C) They smile all the time.

      (D) They enjoy being bullied.

(   ) 3. Which of the following is mentioned in the poster as a way of bullying?

      (A) Make someone laugh in the class.

      (B) Report bullying behavior to a teacher.

      (C) Stop a little boy beating another little girl.

      (D) Say cruel things about people on the Internet.

(   ) 4. Who might be the target readers of the poster?

      (A) Students.   (B) Teachers.

      (C) Parents.   (D) Bullies.

(   ) 5. Which of the following can be inferred from the poster?

      (A) Bullies usually look angry and scary.

      (B) Bullying won't stop if people keep silent.

      (C) Bullying among children is just a harmless game.

      (D) Most people have the experience of being bullied.

Vocabulary & Phrases

1. **bullying** [`bʊliɪŋ] *n.* [U] 霸凌問題

   * Bullying can happen to anyone and happen anywhere. We must learn how to protect ourselves.

   bully [`bʊlɪ] *n.* [C] 霸凌者 | *vt.* 恐嚇，霸凌

   * Bullies sometimes bully others just for fun.

   * Don't let them bully you into doing anything you don't want to.

2. **have sth. in common** 有相同的… (興趣、特點)

   * Although Miguel and I have nothing in common, we are still best friends.

3. **comment** [`kɑmɛnt] *n.* [C] 評論

   * The mayor refused to make any comments on the news.

4. **nasty** [`næstɪ] *adj.* 惡意的

   * You shouldn't have made nasty remarks about others.

5. **nightmare** [`naɪt‚mɛr] *n.* [C] 惡夢；夢魘

   * That horror movie gave me a nightmare last night.

6. **put an end to sth.** 使終止

   * The teacher put an end to the quarrel between the two students.

7. **Enough is enough.** 夠了 (認爲不應再繼續)

   * Enough is enough. I am tired of your excuses.

8. **identify** [aɪ`dɛntə‚faɪ] *vt.* 辨別

   * The dead man was identified as the famous movie actor.

➡ Words for Recognition

1. online [ˌɑnˈlaɪn] *adv.* 線上地

➡ Pop Quiz

_____ 1. A well-trained dog can i_____y the smell of drugs.

_____ 2. I didn't sleep well, because I had a n_____e last night.

_____ 3. The two languages have a lot in c_____n.

_____ 4. Most of the c_____ts on the novel are critical.

_____ 5. I don't know why Lisa always makes n_____y remarks about her friends.

Anti-bullying Poster

Respect Copyright

Confused about copyright? Let's check it out.

A copyright symbol usually means something is protected by copyright, and you cannot make copies without permission. It is actually against the law to make a copy of something and use it for business purposes if it is protected by copyright. However, it's permissible to copy a reasonable number of pages for educational purposes. For instance, a teacher could copy a poem from poetry to use in a handout. And a student could make a copy of a newspaper article for a school project. This is known as **fair use**. If you do copy something in this way, always remember to acknowledge the source.

Keep in mind that it is illegal to sell or share copyrighted works, which includes digital editions. You shouldn't break the copyright laws; otherwise you may get into serious trouble.

If you are still unsure about it, contact the copyright owner and ask for permission. Neither ideas nor copyrighted works are free. It's your responsibility to know the rules and follow them.

(   ) 1. What is the main purpose of this passage?

     (A) To explain the origins of the copyright symbol.

     (B) To clarify some common issues related to copyright.

     (C) To encourage people not to use copyrighted materials.

     (D) To teach young people how to get around copyright laws.

(   ) 2. What does the phrase "**fair use**" in the first paragraph most likely mean?

     (A) The idea that it is legal to use part of something for teaching.

     (B) The idea that it is not fair to use those materials without paying.

     (C) The concept that all creative writing should be free to use.

     (D) The laws that protect artists' and authors' works from being used illegally.

(   ) 3. According to the passage, which of the following is true?

     (A) People should contact a lawyer when feeling confused.

     (B) People can't copy materials without copyright symbols.

     (C) The safest way of using other's work is to contact its owner.

     (D) The copyright symbol warns people not to copy any material at all.

(   ) 4. Which of the following is NOT protected by copyright?

     (A) A newspaper article.

     (B) A poem printed in poetry.

     (C) A chapter from a published novel.

     (D) A shopping list written by your mother.

(   ) 5. What does the author mean by the last sentence of the passage?

     (A) It's everyone's job to know and respect the copyright laws.

     (B) It's terrible when people break the copyright laws by copying things.

     (C) You should always assume that you are watched by copyright lawyers.

     (D) It's our duty to contact the police whenever copyright laws are broken.

1. **copyright** [ˋkɑpɪˏraɪt] *n.* [C][U] 著作權 | *adj.* 受版權保護的 | *vt.* 獲得···版權

   * All the articles in the magazine are protected by copyright.

   * It is illegal to use copyright materials without the owner's permission.

   * The author has copyrighted her new book.

2. **permissible** [pɚˋmɪsəbl̩] *adj.* 允許的

   * It isn't permissible to enter the building without an employee ID card.

3. **acknowledge** [əkˋnɑlɪdʒ] *vt.* 註明

   * You must acknowledge sources of the information you used in the essay.

4. **digital** [ˋdɪdʒɪtl̩] *adj.* 數位式的

   * Digital cameras allow people to see the photos before printing them.

5. **clarify** [ˋklærəˏfaɪ] *vt.* 澄清，闡明

   * The research will help us to clarify the problem.

6. **material** [məˋtɪrɪəl] *n.* [C][U] 資料

   * You have to collect all the relevant materials before doing the experiment.

7. **get around** 避開

   * Keep getting around the problem won't help you solve it.

8. **concept** [ˋkɑnsɛpt] *n.* [C] 概念，觀念

   * It is hard for a little girl to understand the concept of death.

9. **publish** [ˋpʌblɪʃ] *vt.* 出版

   * All of the writer's books have been published as e-books.

10. **assume** [əˋsum] *vt.* 假定

    * I always assume the worst. It helps me prepare for every situation.

➤ Words for Recognition

1. handout [`hænd͵aʊt] *n.* [C] 講義

➤ Pop Quiz

_____ 1. The teacher uses some movies as her teaching m_____l.

_____ 2. The mayor refused to c_____y if she is for or against this issue.

_____ 3. The central c_____t of the essay is love.

_____ 4. Andrea is excited that her story was p_____hed in the newspaper.

_____ 5. It is not p_____e for people to smoke in public areas.

Unit 18

Save the Dogs!

Location: King's Park
Date: Sat. 4/7, Sun. 4/8   Time: 10:00–16:00

Come on! Pet and play with as many as 50 dogs and puppies that are in desperate need of a family. There are dogs of all sizes and characters to suit all kinds of households and each dog has been neutered and is parasite-free. We will also provide workshops, giving expert advice on training and caring for your new **fellows**.

Each day a lottery will be held for anyone who donates to Pray for the Strays foundation with the chance to win a variety of dog accessories, including dog beds and high-quality dog food.

– Up to 50 dogs are ready to be adopted
   Registration Fee: 1. Microchip implant-NT$ 250
                      2. Rabies vaccine-NT$ 300
– Workshops on how to care for your new pets
– Lottery each day
– Handmade dog accessories and toys for sale
– Delicious hot dogs

Why buy a new puppy when there are so many dogs already in need of your help?
The perfect pet is waiting for you to take it home.

Organized by Pray for the Strays
Email: prayforstrays@gmail.com

(   ) 1. What is this event mainly about?

      (A) Lottery.

      (B) Dog adoption.

      (C) Praying for the strays.

      (D) Selling pet accessories.

(   ) 2. What is the purpose of the workshops?

      (A) How to raise the pets.

      (B) How to help stray dogs.

      (C) How to make dog collars and toys.

      (D) How to help the dog receive the vaccine.

(   ) 3. What do "**fellows**" in the first paragraph refer to?

      (A) The hot dog sellers.

      (B) The staff of workshops.

      (C) The dogs that are adopted.

      (D) The donors of the event.

(   ) 4. What information is NOT listed in the leaflet?

      (A) Contact information.

      (B) Time and place.

      (C) Organizer and activities.

      (D) Entrance fee.

(   ) 5. What should you do first if you want to win the dog accessories?

      (A) Adopt a dog.   (B) Buy hot dogs.

      (C) Attend the workshop.   (D) Donate to the organization.

Words for Recognition

1. **desperate** [ˈdɛspərɪt] *adj.* 非常嚴重的；極端的

   ＊After the serious typhoon, the victims' houses are in desperate need of repair.

2. **workshop** [ˈwɜ˞kˌʃɑp] *n.* [C] 工作坊

   ＊The non-governmental organization offered a photography workshop to its workers.

3. **lottery** [ˈlɑtərɪ] *n.* [C] 抽獎；彩券

   ＊What would you do if you win the lottery?

4. **donate** [doˈnet] *vi.* / *vt.* 捐贈，捐助

   ＊My company donated over 3,000 new computers to local schools.

   donor [ˈdonə˞] *n.* [C] 捐助者，捐贈者

   ＊The church received one million dollars from a generous donor.

5. **stray** [stre] *n.* [C] 流浪動物 | *adj.* 流浪的，走失的

   ＊Kevin is an animal lover. His dream is to provide a shelter for the strays / stray dogs.

6. **foundation** [faʊnˈdeʃən] *n.* [C] 基金會

   ＊The aim of the foundation is to help people who cannot find a job.

7. **accessory** [ækˈsɛsərɪ] *n.* [C] 配件，附屬品

   ＊The shop in downtown sells all kinds of fashion accessories like earrings and rings.

8. **vaccine** [ˈvækˌsin] *n.* [C][U] 疫苗

   ＊The experts are worried that there is no vaccine against the new disease.

9. **organizer** [ˈɔrgənaɪzə˞] *n.* [C] 籌辦者

   ＊The organizer has prepared 100 gifts for the participants.

Words for Recognition

1. neuter [`njutɚ] *vt.* 去勢，結紮
2. parasite [`pærəˌsaɪt] *n.* [C] 寄生蟲
3. microchip [`maɪkroˌtʃɪp] *n.* [C] 晶片
4. implant [`ɪmplænt] *n.* [C][U] 移植物，植入物
5. rabies [`rebiz] *n.* [U] 狂犬病
6. adoption [ə`dɑpʃən] *n.* [C][U] 收養

Pop Quiz

_____ 1. Bruce had won the l____y and became a millionaire.

_____ 2. The f____n provides several scholarships for students in need every year.

_____ 3. Although Amelia lives on a small salary, she still insists on d____ting to the charity every month.

_____ 4. There's a d____e need of food, water, and medical supplies in the refugee camps.

_____ 5. The problem of the s____ys on the streets can't be solved in a short time because there are too many of them.

Unit 19
Tune in Tonight and Learn About Human Rights!

 Peace X Human Right

Just now · 🌐

Human rights are fragile. So even if you live in a free country that values the rights of humans, human rights will always be an important issue to discuss.

This is why we are happy to announce that we will be hosting a series of five lectures on human rights over the course of the week. Each lecture will be two hours in length, starting at 7:30 pm and will be broadcast on Facebook Live.

Our first speaker is the famous professor of law at UCLA and human rights activist, Geoffrey Tate. He is well-known for his crucial role in many important law cases involving the **First Amendment**. From his experience, Professor Tate will be speaking tonight on the importance of freedom of speech in society. A truly dedicated activist, Geoffrey continually campaigns for human rights, especially in terms of freedom of speech.

Be sure to tune in to our Facebook Live at 7:30 this evening. Don't forget to like and share this post to have the chance of receiving a free Human Rights coaster.

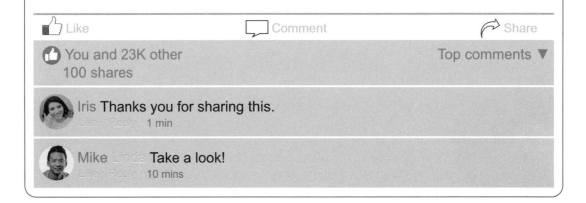

👍 Like   💬 Comment   ↗ Share

👍 You and 23K other   Top comments ▼
100 shares

Iris **Thanks you for sharing this.**
Like · Reply · 1 min

Mike ___ **Take a look!**
Like · Reply · 10 mins

( ) 1. How many speeches in total will there be and which one is the one mentioned in the passage?

(A) 5, first.   (B) 5, second.   (C) 4, first.   (D) 4, last.

( ) 2. At what time will the lectures end?

(A) 7:30.   (B) 19:30.   (C) 9: 30.   (D) 21:30.

( ) 3. What does "**First Amendment**" in the third paragraph most likely refer to?

(A) The right to privacy.   (B) A school policy.

(C) A degree in law.   (D) A law regarding free speech.

( ) 4. What do people need to do in order to win a free coaster?

(A) Like and share the post.

(B) Tune in to Facebook Live of the lectures.

(C) Leave comments during the broadcast.

(D) Watch all the speeches and answer the questions.

( ) 5. According to the post, which of the following statements is true?

(A) In developed countries, people enjoy greater freedom, and don't really need to care about human rights.

(B) Whichever country or region people live in, they should care about the issue of human rights.

(C) Geoffrey is very glad to see the courses on social justice take people by storm and get positive feedback.

(D) Geoffrey is an excellent expert in the field of human rights; without him, the First Amendment would never be passed.

Unit 19

Vocabulary & Phrases

1. **fragile** [`frædʒəl] *adj.* 易損壞的；脆弱的

   ＊The military exercises may cause serious damage to the fragile relationship between the two countries.

2. **host** [host] *vt.* 主辦，主持

   ＊It is said that the new talk show will be hosted by Madonna.

3. **lecture** [`lɛktʃɚ] *n.* [C] 講座

   ＊Many students are willing to attend the series of lectures on pop music.

4. **over the course of sth.** 在⋯的期間

   ＊Over the course of the meeting, the two companies have reached an agreement.

5. **(time) in length** 為 (時) 多久

   ＊The horror movie is 125 minutes in length.

6. **professor** [prə`fɛsɚ] *n.* [C] 教授

   ＊Maria is a professor of chemistry at Harvard University.

7. **activist** [`æktɪvɪst] *n.* [C] (政治、社會性的) 活躍份子

   ＊Paul is an animal rights activist.

8. **crucial** [`kruʃəl] *adj.* 關鍵的

   ＊Winning this contract is crucial to the company's future.

9. **dedicated** [`dɛdəketɪd] *adj.* 盡心盡力的，盡職盡責的

   ＊The dedicated vet devoted most of her lifetime to helping the strays.

10. **campaign** [kæm`pen] *vi.* 從事活動，發起運動

    ＊The environmentalists are campaigning against nuclear power.

11. **globe** [glob] *n.* [C] 世界

    ＊My dream is to travel around the globe and visit more than 100 countries.

12. **tune in (to)** 收聽 (廣播)；收看 (電視)

    ＊"Don't forget to tune in to *News for You* with Tammy at 7 p.m.," the host said.

13. **privacy** [ˋpraɪvəsɪ] *n.* [U] 隱私

　　＊As a public figure, it is hard for him to enjoy complete privacy.

14. **regarding** [rɪˋgɑrdɪŋ] *prep.* 關於

　　＊My teacher told me to contact her if I have any problems regarding the research.

15. **feedback** [ˋfidˏbæk] *n.* [U] 意見回饋

　　＊Most the feedback from our customers is positive.

▶ Words for Recognition

1. Facebook Live 臉書直播：社群網站 Facebook 開放的線上直播功能。藉由網路，使用者可於行動裝置及電腦上進行實況轉播。
2. UCLA 加州大學洛杉磯分校：位於美國加州洛杉磯的一所公立大學。
3. First Amendment 美國憲法第一修正案：確立四項基本自由權 (宗教信仰和活動自由、言論自由、出版自由及和平集會與請願自由權)。
4. coaster [ˋkostɚ] *n.* 杯墊

▶ Pop Quiz

_____ 1. The actress's p_____y is invaded by reporters and paparazzi.

_____ 2. Be careful! The vase is very f_____e and may be damaged easily.

_____ 3. The decision you made is c_____l to the result of the whole plan.

_____ 4. Let's t_____e in to *Friday Night*. My favorite actor is on the show!

_____ 5. People are c_____ning to save these historic buildings from being torn down.

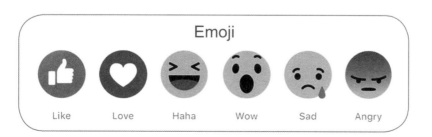

Tune in Tonight and Learn About Human Rights!　　77

Unit 20
Single Stories and Stereotypes

When the Nigerian author, Chimamanda Ngozi Adichie, went to study at a university in the United States, her roommate was surprised that she knew how to use a stove. Chimamanda soon realized that her roommate had a single story of Africa. In her well-known TED talk, Chimamanda explains the danger of the single story: "The single story creates stereotypes, and the problem with stereotypes is not that they are untrue, but that they are incomplete. They make one story become the only story."

Whether we like it or not, we all have single stories about the world around us. As a white foreigner in Taiwan, I have experienced this myself. For some strange reason that I have never quite understood, Taiwanese people often assume that I am an American. It's the single story of a white person living in Taiwan. When I explain that I am from England, the single story is then replaced by another involving fog, rain, London, and gentlemen, i.e., a bunch of simple stereotypes associated with my home country. You may wonder what my single story of Taiwan was before I arrived here in 1993. In fact, I knew virtually nothing about this country other than it was well-known for producing cheap goods. Unfortunately, even though this single story of Taiwan is no longer true, it persists in the minds of many people who are unfamiliar with Taiwan's achievements in the past few decades.

How are we to avoid the danger of a single story? The key is to examine one's own beliefs about the world and other people. Look beyond the stereotypes and only then will they start to disappear.

(　　) 1. Why was Chimamanda's roommate surprised to learn that she knew how to use a stove?

    (A) She had difficulty with the language barrier.

    (B) She was just making a joke to break the ice.

    (C) She was hoping that someone would teach her how to cook.

    (D) She probably thought people in Africa did not have stoves.

(　　) 2. What is the second paragraph mainly about?

    (A) The author's initial conception of Taiwan.

    (B) The author's personal experience of cultural stereotypes.

    (C) The author's anger at the misconceptions about England.

    (D) The traditional stories that the author had read in Taiwan.

(　　) 3. According to the passage, what is the single story of Taiwan?

    (A) It's a nation that manufactures cheap goods.

    (B) It's a small island with a rich cultural heritage.

    (C) It's one of the most advanced industrial countries in Asia.

    (D) It is a place that is always covered in a blanket of fog.

(　　) 4. Which of the following about Chimamanda is NOT true?

    (A) She is not a white foreigner in Taiwan.

    (B) She received her higher education in America.

    (C) She learned how to light the stove in America.

    (D) She gave a speech on the danger of the single story.

(　　) 5. Where does the author of this passage currently live?

    (A) Nigeria.   (B) Taiwan.

    (C) The United States.   (D) The United Kingdom.

Vocabulary & Phrases

1. **stereotype** [`stɛrɪə,taɪp] *n.* [C] 刻板印象

   * We can find many examples of gender stereotypes in traditional fairy tales.

2. **university** [,junə`vɝsətɪ] *n.* [C][U] 大學

   * John decides to study law at university.

3. **virtually** [`vɝtʃʊəlɪ] *adv.* 實質上地；幾乎

   * The vacuum cleaner can virtually remove all the dust on the ground.

4. **other than** 不同於，除了 (常用於否定句)

   * The document cannot be read by anyone other than the manager.

5. **goods** [gʊdz] *n. pl.* 商品

   * There are twenty percent discount on all the goods during the year-end sale.

6. **persist** [pɚ`sɪst] *vi. / vt.* 執意，留存

   * The little boy persists in buying the toy.

7. **initial** [ɪ`nɪʃəl] *adj.* 最初的

   * To be honest, my initial impression of Roy was that he was a shy man.

8. **conception** [kən`sɛpʃən] *n.* [C][U] 見解，想法

   * People from different social backgrounds have different conceptions of happiness.

9. **manufacture** [,mænjə`fæktʃɚ] *vt.* 製造

   * The cars which are manufactured in the factory will be exported to the US.

10. **heritage** [`hɛrətɪdʒ] *n.* [U] 文化遺產

    * It is everyone's responsibility to preserve the national heritage.

11. **prejudice** [`prɛdʒədɪs] *n.* [C] 偏見

    * The organization aims to overcome prejudice against women in the workplace.

Words for Recognition

1. Nigerian [naɪˋdʒɪrɪən] *adj.* 奈及利亞人；奈及利亞的
2. Africa 非洲：位於東半球西部，地跨赤道南北，是世界面積第二大洲，也是人口第二大洲。
3. TED talk TED 演講：TED 指 Technology, Entertainment, Design (技術、娛樂、設計)，講者針對相關議題演說，公開於網站供民眾觀看。
4. i.e. [ˌaɪˋi] *abbr.* 也就是 (源自拉丁文 id est [ˌɪdˋɛst])

Pop Quiz

_____ 1. My brother works for a factory m_____ring furniture.

_____ 2. I have no c_____n of what babies really want.

_____ 3. In the i_____l stage of the disease, most patients feel dizzy.

_____ 4. The reporter p_____ted in asking questions about the election.

_____ 5. V_____y all my classmates go to cram schools after school.

Unit 21
Taiwan's Indigenous Languages Are Disappearing

Around 400 years ago, people from China traveled across the sea to Taiwan to start a new life. At the time, Taiwan had a relatively small population of indigenous people. Collectively, they spoke 42 languages, but as the years went by, the number of people who could speak these languages decreased. Today, nine of the original 42 languages are in danger of disappearing forever.

Language and culture go hand in hand. When a minority culture is influenced by another more dominant culture, its language will become threatened. This is a trend that is occurring all over the world. In some regions, only a handful of people can speak a particular language. When they pass away, the language will die if it has not been passed on to a younger generation. For example, the Sakizaya tribe in Taiwan has a population of less than seven hundred. Its native language is under threat because so few people speak it. The Council of Indigenous Peoples in Taiwan has been working hard to prevent the death of these languages. The loss would not just be language but culture, because these languages often convey useful knowledge about local plants and animals.

Taiwan is exploring different ways of preserving these endangered languages. One of the challenges is to figure out a writing system so that learners do not have to rely solely on the spoken word. Let's hope that researchers can carry out **this important work**.

(   ) 1. Which of the following best describes the author's attitude toward the preservation of indigenous languages?

(A) Concerned.   (B) Defensive.   (C) Negative.   (D) Optimistic.

(   ) 2. According to the passage, which of the following is true about the Sakizaya tribe?

(A) Its language might soon be extinct.

(B) Plants and animals there are extinct.

(C) People there don't protect its language.

(D) Nine of their languages are in danger of disappearing.

(   ) 3. According to the passage, besides the cultural reasons, why are indigenous languages so important?

(A) They can attract tourists to Taiwan.

(B) They can prevent death and disease.

(C) They contain information about local wildlife.

(D) They help raise funds for the Council of Indigenous Peoples.

(   ) 4. What does "**this important work**" in the last paragraph refer to?

(A) Finding a way to profit from this difficult situation.

(B) Developing a universal language to share knowledge.

(C) Protecting the land that was taken from the indigenous people.

(D) Creating a system to write down and conserve indigenous languages.

(   ) 5. From which of the following is the passage most likely to be taken?

(A) A business journal.   (B) A science magazine.

(C) A guide to language learning.   (D) A book on aboriginal culture.

➤ Vocabulary & Phrases

1. **relatively** [`rɛlətɪvlɪ] *adv.* 相對地；比較上

   ＊Some students think that this book is relatively hard to understand.

2. **collectively** [kə`lɛktɪvlɪ] *adv.* 共同地

   ＊All the family members are collectively responsible for the housework.

3. **decrease** [dɪ`kris] *vi. / vt.* 減少

   ＊The doctor asked the patient to decrease the calories he took in.

4. **go hand in hand (with sth.)** 和…息息相關

   ＊A student's success goes hand in hand with the effort he or she has put in.

5. **dominant** [`dɑmənənt] *adj.* 主要的；優勢的

   ＊We can't deny that the United States still plays a dominant role in the world.

6. **council** [`kaʊnsl̩] *n.* [C] 委員會

   ＊This study is supported by the Medical Research Council.

7. **convey** [kən`ve] *vt.* 傳達；運送

   ＊The book conveys an important message to young people: "Work hard, play harder."

8. **explore** [ɪk`splor] *vt.* 探索研究

   ＊The doctors are exploring the possibility of curing the serious illness.

9. **preserve** [prɪ`zɝv] *vt.* 保存，維護

   ＊The library has preserved many valuable old books.

10. **endangered** [ɪn`dendʒɚd] *adj.* 瀕危的；瀕臨絕種的

    ＊We must do something, or more and more animals will become endangered species.

11. **solely** [`sollɪ] *adv.* 唯一地

    ＊According to the police, the driver is not solely responsible for the car accident.

12. **researcher** [rɪ`sɝtʃɚ] *n.* [C] 研究員

    ＊Researchers have found that people who exercise regularly live longer.

13. **carry out** 完成 (任務)

＊Ethan Hunt has once again carried out the mission successfully.

14. **preservation** [ˌprɛzɚˋveʃən] *n.* [U] 保護；維護

＊The preservation of rain forest is important.

15. **wildlife** [ˋwaɪldˌlaɪf] *n.* [U] 野生動物

＊In order to protect wildlife, the government establishes a nature preservation.

16. **universal** [ˌjunəˋvɝsl] *adj.* 普遍的，全世界的

＊"Money can't buy happiness," is a universal truth.

17. **conserve** [kənˋsɝv] *vt.* 保護，保存

＊We can conserve water by flushing the toilet with waste water.

Words for Recognition

1. indigenous [ɪnˋdɪdʒənəs] *adj.* 本地的，土生土長的
2. Sakizaya 撒奇萊雅族：臺灣原住民的其中一個族群，世居於花蓮。

Pop Quiz

_____ 1. The government has been working on the preservation of e____d species.

_____ 2. As we know, climate change is one of the u____l problems we must deal with.

_____ 3. Mary's letter c____yed a great sense of regret.

_____ 4. The professor e____red how human bodies will function under different drugs.

_____ 5. Some experts are worried because the birth rate in Taiwan is d____sing.

Unit 22
Priority Seating: *Yea or Nay*

The following is an excerpt from an interview.

Host:

Priority seats on public transportation are typically reserved for those with special needs, such as the elderly, the impaired, pregnant women and passengers with children. However, a few incidents have highlighted some problems of priority seats. In one case, a blind man was harassed for sitting on a priority seat because he didn't look visibly impaired. Moreover, a young lady was also criticized for sitting on the priority seat. But the truth is that she is three months pregnant. Incidents like these have led the public to protest against the priority seats. There is also a petition of almost 7000 signatures calling for the removal of priority seats in the public transportation systems. Professor Lee, what is your opinion on this subject?

Professor Lee:

Well, it seems to me that it is an overreaction. After all, the purpose of priority seats is to offer seats to those in need. This is a case of **throwing the baby out with the bathwater**.

Host:

Interesting points, but what about those who are not elderly, impaired, or pregnant? They may have special needs, too. Don't you think the policy of priority seats is discriminating against those people?

Professor Lee:

Public transportation can't be perfect for everyone. But I would argue that the good of priority seats does outweigh any potential harm. Sure, the system needs improving, but just as I have said, destroying it entirely is a bit over the top. I would also like to mention that this is more of a communication problem. If people could communicate more and make their needs be known to others, then some conflicts can probably be avoided.

Host:

It's just hard for some people to express their needs in public, and maybe that's why these incidents occur. Okay. That's all the time we have for today. Let's agree to disagree. Professor Lee, thank you for sharing your opinions with us.

(   ) 1. What is the professor's position on the removal of priority seats?

    (A) For it.   (B) Against it.   (C) Neutral.   (D) Indifferent.

(   ) 2. Which of the following incident had caused the public to call for the removal of priority seats?

    (A) A blind man falsely accused by others.

    (B) A pregnant woman yielding her seat to the elderly.

    (C) A public protest against the priority seats.

    (D) A government's new policy on priority seats.

(   ) 3. What does **"throwing the baby out with the bathwater"** in the professor's first response most likely mean?

    (A) To keep a bad idea because of a minor advantage.

    (B) To keep a good idea because it has many advantages.

    (C) To get rid of a bad idea because of its disadvantages.

    (D) To get rid of a good idea because of a minor disadvantage.

(   ) 4. What does the host mean by his conclusion of the interview?

    (A) The public transportation bureau should make decisions.

    (B) The host will invite a government official from the transportation bureau to be a guest.

    (C) The host and professor Lee may have different opinions on priority seats, but they respect one another.

    (D) The minority should obey the majority, so let the public decide whether to keep or remove priority seats.

(   ) 5. What can be inferred from the interview?

    (A) The host and the professor agree to remove priority seats.

    (B) The purpose of the interview is to discuss the public safety.

    (C) Public transportation is designed for the elderly and the impaired.

    (D) Professor Lee thinks that the real problem is communication, not priority seats.

Vocabulary & Phrases

1. **host** [host] *n.* [C] 主持人

   ＊The host of the new talk show might be Emma, the rising star.

2. **pregnant** [`prɛgnənt] *adj.* 懷孕的

   ＊It is important for a pregnant woman to have a balanced diet.

3. **incident** [`ɪnsədənt] *n.* [C] (不好的) 事件

   ＊More than 150 violent incidents was reported last year.

4. **highlight** [`haɪ‚laɪt] *vt.* 強調；使醒目

   ＊Such an accident highlights the importance of seat belts.

5. **harass** [hə`ræs] *vt.* 騷擾

   ＊Susan complained of being sexually harassed by the manager.

6. **protest** [prə`tɛst] *vi. / vt.* 抗議｜[`protɛst] *n.* [C][U] 抗議

   ＊Many people are protesting against nuclear power.

   ＊The policy raised a storm of protest among the students.

7. **signature** [`sɪgnətʃɚ] *n.* [C] 簽名

   ＊The bank clerk asked me to put my signature to the form.

8. **removal** [rɪ`muvl̩] *n.* [C][U] 去除

   ＊The removal of trade barriers can help economy.

9. **discriminate** [dɪ`skrɪmə‚net] *vi.* 歧視，差別待遇

   ＊Some of the parents still discriminate against girls and are in favor of boys.

10. **throw the baby out with the bathwater**

    把嬰兒和洗澡水一起倒掉，不分好壞全都丟棄

    ＊Don't throw the baby out with the bathwater, or you may lose the golden chance.

11. **potential** [pə`tɛnʃəl] *adj.* 潛在的

    ＊What are the potential dangers of traveling alone?

12. **over the top** 過頭，過火

    ＊Jake's joke is totally over the top. Some of his friends are mad at him.

13. **communication** [kə͵mjunəˋkeʃən] *n.* [U] 溝通

    ＊Good communication between teachers and students is important.

14. **bureau** [ˋbjʊro] *n.* [C] 局，處

    ＊The transportation bureau is working on the traffic noise.

15. **accuse** [əˋkjuz] *vt.* 譴責；控告

    ＊You can't accuse someone without proof.

16. **destruction** [dɪˋstrʌkʃən] *n.* [U] 破壞

    ＊The destruction of the rainforests is an important issue.

17. **disadvantage** [͵dɪsədˋvæntɪdʒ] *n.* [C] 不利因素

    ＊Shyness might be a disadvantage of being a salesperson.

➤ Words for Recognition

1. yea or nay 是或否

2. impaired [ɪmˋpɛrd] *adj.* 有缺陷的

3. petition [pəˋtɪʃən] *n.* [C] 請願書

➤ Pop Quiz

_____ 1. In order to attract p_____l customers, the restaurant decided to offer a wide variety of foods.

_____ 2. Some people had been d_____ted against merely because of their weight.

_____ 3. The workers held a peaceful p_____t against the unfair policy.

_____ 4. The man was caught by the police officer and a_____ed of murder.

_____ 5. The shy and silent boy has little c_____n with others.

Unit 23

Relocation Notice

Mamma Mia is Moving!

We have found a new home at 244 Sherman Street!

Just two blocks away. See the map below for more detailed directions!

New! | Cadbury Road | Upland Road

Sherman Street

The new location has:

♻ A second floor for private parties or other events.

♻ It owns parking lot with spaces for 26 cars. Just right next door!

♻ An amazing enlarged new kitchen for the expanded menu.

　We offer all of your old favorites and more specials now!

♻ New brick oven! Fresh bread and pizza every day!

🔊 The last day party is on Sat. April 8th.

　All the diners can get a free drink of their choice! (Wine or soft drinks)

🔊 The grand reopening will be on Fri. April 28th.

　A very special secret guest will attend. And of course, there would be special offers. Visit our fan page for more details of the reopening day.

www.mammamiarestaurant.com

We truly appreciate you, our loyal customers.

Thanks to you, Mamma Mia has become a part of our amazing community.

Mamma Mia

(   ) 1. What is the purpose of this notice?

(A) To promote the restaurant by special offers.

(B) To welcome the diners to taste the new specials.

(C) To inform the customers of the changes of Mamma Mia.

(D) To announce the opening of new branch at Sherman Street.

(   ) 2. According to the notice, where will be the parking lot of Mamma Mia?

(A) It is right beside the restaurant.

(B) It is just one block away.

(C) It is located in the back of the restaurant.

(D) It is right across the road in front of the restaurant.

(   ) 3. What is mentioned about the new kitchen in the notice?

(A) It is not ideal.   (B) It is much bigger.

(C) It cost a lot to build.   (D) It doesn't have an oven.

(   ) 4. What can diners expect at the new location?

(A) Freshly baked bread.   (B) A younger chef.

(C) Higher menu prices.   (D) Fewer dishes on the menu.

(   ) 5. Which of the following about the old location of Mamma Mia can be inferred from the notice?

(A) It provides more seating for diners.

(B) It is a one-story restaurant.

(C) It is going to become a fashion store.

(D) It is superior to the new one.

Vocabulary & Phrases

1. **enlarge** [ɪnˋlɑrdʒ] *vi. / vt.* 放大；擴增

   ＊The company decided to enlarge its factory from one story to three stories.

2. **expand** [ɪkˋspænd] *vi. / vt.* 擴大；膨脹

   ＊The number of shortsighted students is expanding, so almost everyone is wearing glasses.

3. **loyal** [ˋlɔɪəl] *adj.* 忠實的，忠誠的

   ＊Dogs are considered to be human's loyal friends.

4. **thanks to sb. / sth.** 幸虧⋯，由於⋯

   ＊The refugee camps are finally done, thanks to the help from the public.

5. **community** [kəˋmjunətɪ] *n.* [C] 社區

   ＊Having good community relations is important to crime prevention.

6. **brand new** [͵brændˋnju] *adj.* 嶄新的

   ＊I build a brand new doghouse for my puppy.

7. **chef** [ʃɛf] *n.* [C] 廚師

   ＊Mr. Lin is one of the top chefs in Asia; his restaurant is always full.

Words for Recognition

1. special [ˋspɛʃəl] *n.* [C] 特色菜
2. diner [ˋdaɪnɚ] *n.* [C] 用餐者，食客

Pop Quiz

_____ 1. Could you e_____e the text on the screen for me? I can't read them.

_____ 2. Lesley bought a b_____d new car and couldn't wait to show off.

_____ 3. My grandfather knows almost everyone in this c_____y because he has lived here for sixty years.

_____ 4. The company e_____ds the business by offering online shopping.

_____ 5. Jack has been a l_____l customer to the company for years.

常見地點

1.超市	6.醫院	11.公園	16.公車站
2.劇院	7.學校	12.加油站	17.電影院
3.體育場	8.博物館	13.飯店	18.藥局
4.消防局	9.銀行	14.警察局	19.咖啡店
5.紅綠燈	10.郵局	15.公車總站	20.十字路口

常用方向

 Make a U-turn 迴轉   Go straight 直走

 Turn Left 左轉   Turn Right 右轉

Choose Me for Fal Tech

Sammy Brock

1705 Murphy Road, Venice, CA 90291

Phone: 1−802−5551234

E-mail: sammybrock@sanminmail.com

Feb. 23, 2018

Chloe Robinson

Hiring manager

Fal Tech

58 Ethanac Road,

Los Angeles, CA 90024

Dear Ms. Robinson,

As an experienced software engineer, I understand the importance of innovation in software development, especially at the cutting edge that Fal Tech places itself in the market. Fal Tech pushes things forward and I can help to push them further for Fal Tech.

Why Fal Tech

When it comes to new software developers today, Fal Tech is certainly the leading company. And nothing can beat the fresh environment of a ringing start-up that encourages creativity and gives its employees the freedom in the pursuit of their own ideas. That is why I am eager to be a part of this growing company.

My Experience

After graduating from Stanford University with a degree in computer science, I have worked for many prominent software companies in various roles.

- At Ensemble, I headed the development of its cloud database.
- At Obisoft, I designed the networking code for the massively multiplayer online role-playing games (MMORPG), *Dark Horizon* .

I am technically skilled in both database and networking systems and I am good at 12 programming languages.

Why me

Coding is my life. Nothing is more pleasing than working in a team toward a common goal, slowly but surely turning nothing into something of value. As such, I understand not only what it takes to get results but perhaps more importantly also what doesn't get results. I pride myself on being able to stir myself and others to go the extra mile. I am a firm believer in striving for excellence in every endeavor.

Sincerely,
Sammy Brock

Unit 24

(　　) 1. What is the tone of this passage?
　　　　(A) Pessimistic.　　　　　　(B) Cautious.
　　　　(C) Humble.　　　　　　　(D) Passionate.

(　　) 2. What does the author say about Fal Tech?
　　　　(A) It is a branch of Obisoft.
　　　　(B) It is a rising star in the industry.
　　　　(C) It is an old company in the industry.
　　　　(D) It is good at producing computers.

(　　) 3. What is the author good at?
　　　　(A) Computer programming.　　(B) Game playing.
　　　　(C) Foreign language learning.　(D) Company developing.

(   ) 4. According to the passage, which of the following is true about the author?

    ⒜ He is not great at coding.

    ⒝ He can speak 12 foreign languages.

    ⒞ His attitude toward the job is very active.

    ⒟ He had worked for Ensemble and carried out weather research.

(   ) 5. What is the passage most likely to be?

    ⒜ A story.   ⒝ A cover letter.

    ⒞ An advertisement.   ⒟ A newspaper article.

▶ Vocabulary & Phrases

1. **software** [ˋsɔftˌwɛr] *n.* [U] 軟體

   ＊My computer is too old to run the new software.

2. **innovation** [ˌɪnəˋveʃən] *n.* [U] 創新

   ＊The innovation in smartphone technology helps the company make a fortune.

3. **creativity** [ˌkrieˋtɪvətɪ] *n.* [U] 創造力

   ＊Creativity is very important in the advertising industry.

4. **pursuit** [pɚˋsut] *n.* [U] 追求

   ＊The dishonest company breaks the law in pursuit of profit.

5. **prominent** [ˋprɑmənənt] *adj.* 著名的，重要的

   ＊Newton plays a prominent role in modern physics.

6. **horizon** [həˋraɪzn̩] *n. sing.* 地平線

   ＊We have been to Alishan and watched the sun rising above the horizon.

7. **as such** 嚴格來說

   ＊As such, the present isn't expensive, but it is handmade.

8. **get results** 成功

   ＊After years of practicing, Mindy finally gets results and wins the medal.

9. **go the extra mile for sb. / sth.** 加倍努力

   ＊The young couple went the extra mile for their new born baby.

10. **strive** [straɪv] *vi.* 努力 (strive, strove / strived, striven / strived)

    ＊The factory is striving for greater profit.

11. **endeavor** [ɪn`dɛvɚ] *n.* [C][U] 嘗試，努力

    ＊The rescue team made every endeavor to find the missing climbers.

12. **cautious** [`kɔʃəs] *adj.* 小心謹慎的

    ＊The government took a very cautious approach to the issue.

13. **passionate** [`pæʃənɪt] *adj.* 熱誠的

    ＊Mandy has been passionate about basketball since she was little.

Words for Recognition

1. Venice 威尼斯區：美國加利福尼亞州洛杉磯市的一個海濱行政區，以運河、海灘和街頭藝人著稱。

2. CA 加利福尼亞州 (加州)：加州的郵政縮寫，因其別名為「金州」(The Golden State)。加州的英文為 State of California。

3. Los Angeles 洛杉磯：美國加利福尼亞州南部的都市，為加州第一大城。

4. developer [də`vɛləpɚ] *n.* [C] 開發者，研製者

5. start-up [`stɑrt,ʌp] *n.* [C] 新創公司

6. massively multiplayer online role-playing games (MMORPG) 大型多人線上角色扮演遊戲：玩家在虛擬遊戲世界中扮演一個 (以上) 的角色。

7. cover letter 求職信：通常與履歷一同寄送給徵才單位，信件內容簡單說明求職者應徵該職位的動機。

Pop Quiz

_____ 1. I am p____e about cooking and dream to be a chef, so I plan to learn how to cook.

_____ 2. Recent medical i____n has greatly lowered the death rate.

_____ 3. People have been s____ving for the equality between men and women.

_____ 4. Look! The beautiful sunset is over there on the h____n.

_____ 5. People are moving to cities in p____t of more job opportunities.

Unit 25
7 Ways to Ace a Job Interview

Talent, experience and qualifications could mean very little if you can't perform well in job interviews. Here are seven important steps in preparing for job interviews. They will surely give you the edge over the competition.

1. Research the company—Having knowledge of what the organization does and how it works is crucial to answering the interview questions properly.

2. Match your qualification—Know what specific skills the organization is looking for. Show your interviewers that you meet all the requirements for the job and that you understand what the company needs from you in your prospective position.

3. Practice answering common questions — Prepare answers to common interview questions. "What is your greatest strength / weakness?", "Tell me something about yourself.", and "Why should we hire you?" are some of the popular questions. Giving the interviewers good answers is the best way to make a good impression.

4. Know what to wear—Wear smart! Choose the right piece to put on, depending on the company you go to. But never forget to pay attention to grooming and be sure to iron the clothes you choose.

5. Come prepared—Always bring extra copies of your **résumé** on high quality paper along with all your references and a portfolio of your work. A notepad and pen will also come in handy.

6. Be mindful of body language—Be aware of non-verbal cues. Maintain good posture and look confident. Be attentive, but try not to stare.

7. Have questions—Finally, prepare questions to ask. Try not to ask questions that can be easily answered by going to their website or other accessible sources.

Doing these seven things before an interview is a sure way to land the job you have your eye on.

(　　) 1. What is this article mainly about?

    (A) How to give an interview.

    (B) The importance of an interview.

    (C) The pros and cons of an interview.

    (D) Tips for preparing for an interview.

(　　) 2. How the ideas are presented in the article?

    (A) By using numbers and symbols.

    (B) By giving different opinions.

    (C) By listing them one after another.

    (D) By using examples in real-life situations.

(　　) 3. What does the author say about what to wear?

    (A) Dress casually.   (B) Look clean and tidy.

    (C) Wear brightly-colored suits.   (D) Put on the most expensive clothes.

(　　) 4. Which of the following is NOT mentioned as one of the things to bring?

    (A) A portfolio.   (B) The copy of one's identification.

    (C) Pen and paper.   (D) Spare copies of the résumé.

(　　) 5. According to this article, which of the following is one of the things that the interviewee needs to do before an interview?

    (A) Prepare the answers to common questions.

    (B) Prepare the questions whose answers can be found easily.

    (C) Practice how to speak in front of friends or families.

    (D) Practice body language. Learn to stare at the interviewer.

Unit 25

7 Ways to Ace a Job Interview   **99**

Vocabulary & Phrases

1. **ace** [es] *vt.* 表現卓越

   ＊The student aced every test and won the scholarship.

2. **qualification** [ˌkwɑləfəˋkeʃən] *n.* [C] 資歷

   ＊Having related experience is one of the qualifications for the job.

3. **competition** [ˌkɑmpəˋtɪʃən] *n.* [U] 競爭

   ＊Competition for the high-paying job is cutthroat.

4. **prospective** [prəˋspɛktɪv] *adj.* 預期的

   ＊Lisa is the most experienced one among all the prospective employees.

5. **impression** [ɪmˋprɛʃən] *n.* [C] 印象

   ＊Arriving late will create a very bad impression at work.

6. **résumé** [ˌrɛzuˋme] *n.* [C] 履歷

   ＊I have written my résumé in both Chinese and English.

7. **reference** [ˋrɛfərəns] *n.* [C] 推薦函

   ＊My professor agreed to write me a reference.

8. **non-verbal** [ˌnɑnˋvɝbḷ] *adj.* 非語言的

   ＊Body language is one of the non-verbal ways to communicate with others.

9. **cue** [kju] *n.* [C] 提示

   ＊The dancer is waiting for the cue to get on the stage.

10. **posture** [ˋpɑstʃɚ] *n.* [C][U] 姿勢

    ＊The doctor told me that my neck pain results from my bad posture.

11. **accessible** [ækˋsɛsəbḷ] *adj.* 可取得的

    ＊The information about the popular tourist attraction is accessible on the Internet.

12. **have sb's eye on sth.** 想要得到…，看中…

    ＊Derek has had his eye on the car for several months.

13. **identification** [aɪˌdɛntəfəˋkeʃən] *n.* [U] 身分證明

    ＊The security guard asked the visitors to show their identification.

14. **spare** [spɛr] *adj.* 備用的

　＊Just in case, we always hide the spare key under the doormat.

➤ Words for Recognition

1. interviewer [ˋɪntɚˏvjuɚ] *n.* [C] 面試官

2. grooming [ˋgrumɪŋ] *n.* [U] 梳妝，(人的) 打扮

3. portfolio [portˋfolɪˏo] *n.* [C] (求職用) 作品集

4. the pros and cons 事情的利與弊

5. interviewee [ˏɪntɚvjuɚˋi] *n.* [C] 參與面試者

➤ Pop Quiz

_____ 1. There's intense c_____n to get into the top university.

_____ 2. The model changes different p_____es for the cameras.

_____ 3. I got a bad i_____n of that restaurant because of its noisy environment.

_____ 4. Taking care of the p_____e clients is important for a company.

_____ 5. I always prepare s_____e pens and erasers before an exam.

Unit 26
STAR Customer Service

Below are two letters.

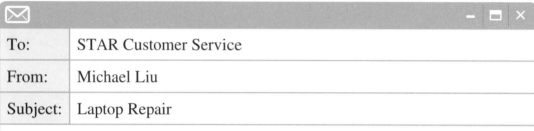

To:	STAR Customer Service
From:	Michael Liu
Subject:	Laptop Repair

Dear STAR Customer Service,

I bought a STAR B120x laptop last year in January. It had been running fine. However, starting a week ago whenever I use it for longer than half an hour, it makes a lot of noise and eventually crashes. I have also noticed that it gets extremely hot. A friend of mine has told me that the laptop is overheating and needs to be repaired.

I find it incredibly upsetting that such an expensive product is having these problems after only one year of use. I expect all the repairs and potential new parts required to be free of charge. My warranty number is 394839375. I hope it can be fixed quickly as I need to use it for my work.

Sincerely yours,

Michael Liu

(   ) 1. What is wrong with Michael's laptop?

     (A) Its battery is dead.   (B) It doesn't start properly.

     (C) It freezes quickly.   (D) It makes noise and crashes.

To:	Michael Liu
From:	STAR Customer Service
Subject:	Re: Laptop Repair

Dear Mr. Liu,

We are sorry to hear that the STAR B120x laptop you purchased on January 10th is not working properly. One of our technicians has reviewed your letter and the problem with your laptop is common and quite repairable.

Unfortunately, we are unable to repair it free of charge as the 12-month warranty on it has expired a month ago. If you would like us to repair the laptop, you will need to take it to any STAR direct store to be inspected.

Please note that the inspection fee is US$25 regardless of whether you choose to repair it or not. We also need to keep your laptop overnight, so our staff can perform the necessary diagnostic tests.

Thank you.

Sincerely,
STAR Customer Service

( ) 2. What is true about the warranty?

    (A) It is still valid.   (B) It has expired.

    (C) Its number is B120x.   (D) It is denied by STAR.

(   ) 3. What can be inferred from the two letters?

        ⑷ STAR customer service is of poor quality.

        ⑻ STAR is able to meet Michael's demands.

        ⑼ Someone from STAR will pick up the broken laptop.

        ⑽ Michael might be disappointed after reading the reply.

(   ) 4. If Michael finds the repair fee unaffordable and decides not to fix after inspection, how much should he pay?

        ⑷ 12 dollars.   ⑻ 25 dollars.

        ⑼ 120 dollars.   ⑽ Free of charge.

(   ) 5. In which month were the two letters most likely to be written?

        ⑷ November.   ⑻ December.

        ⑼ January.   ⑽ February.

▶ Vocabulary & Phrases

1. **eventually** [ɪ`vɛntʃʊəlɪ] *adv.* 最後，終於

 * After years of hard work, Adela was eventually able to buy herself a house.

2. **warranty** [`wɔrəntɪ] *n.* [C] (商品的) 保固，保用卡

 * The company promises a one-year warranty on all types of their products.

3. **technician** [tɛk`nɪʃən] *n.* [C] 技師

 * The technician is so good that she can fix any car within 10 hours.

4. **expire** [ɪk`spaɪr] *vi.* (文件) 到期，期滿

 * My passport expired last week. I need to renew it.

5. **inspect** [ɪn`sɛpkt] *vt.* 檢查；審視

 * The machine has been carefully inspected, so it is safe to use.

 inspection [ɪn`sɛpkʃən] *n.* [C][U] 檢查；視察

 * Under the safety regulation, the elevators need regular inspection.

6. **regardless** [rɪˋgɑrdləss] *adv.* 不管，無論如何

   ＊Everyone is born equal, regardless of race, religion, or sex.

7. **overnight** [͵ovɚˋnaɪt] *adv.* 通宵，整夜

   ＊Because of the bad weather, we are forced to stay overnight at the airport.

8. **valid** [ˋvælɪd] *adj.* 有效的

   ＊The bus ticket is valid for one month.

9. **demand** [dɪˋmænd] *n.* [C] 要求，需求

   ＊One of the company's policies is to meet all the customer's demands.

Words for Recognition

1. faulty [ˋfɔltɪ] *adj.* 有缺陷的
2. laptop [ˋlæp͵tɑp] *n.* [C] 筆記型電腦
3. diagnostic [͵daɪəgˋnɑstɪk] *adj.* 診斷的

Pop Quiz

_____ 1. If your smartphone is still under w____y, the repair of it is free of charge.

_____ 2. I really love northern Chinese dumplings, r____s of meat or vegetable ones.

_____ 3. All sales are final. Please carry out a thorough i____n of the laptop before buying it.

_____ 4. The attendant is willing to meet the customer's d____ds.

_____ 5. I missed the last bus, so I have no choose but to stay at the local hotel o____t.

Unit 27
Upcoming Spring Feast

Below are two letters.

To:	All Employees
From:	Human Resources
Subject:	Spring Dinner Party Survey

Greetings to all employees,

We hope you all enjoyed your Chinese New Year break. To celebrate the start of the new year, we will be holding our spring dinner party within the coming weeks. The date and venue of the event are undecided and will be determined by a vote. Each employee who wishes to attend should state their preferred date and restaurant in their RSVP letter. The restaurants and possible dates are listed below for you to choose from.

Dates: 2/28 (Mon), 3/1 (Tue), 3/2 (Wed), 3/3 (Thu), 3/4 (Fri)

Restaurants:

Chinese	Japanese	American	Italian
Food Palace	The Sushi Bar	Yummy	Pizza Paradise

While the time of the dinner party won't be finalized until the booking is made, it should begin between 6:00 and 8:00 pm.

After the date, time and venue have been confirmed, anyone who wishes to come should notify the department of Human Resources, so we can inform the restaurant about the expected head count.

We apologize in advance to those who won't be able to attend. Thank you.

(   ) 1. What is the purpose of the first letter?

    (A) To see who is coming and who can't make it.

    (B) To have a poll on the dates and venues of a feast.

    (C) To welcome the employees back from the long break.

    (D) To notify the employees of the date and venue of a feast.

✉		− ◻ ✕
To:	All Employees	
From:	Human Resources	
Subject:	Results of Spring Dinner Party Survey	

Attention all employees,

The results of our spring dinner party vote are in and the date and restaurant have been decided.

It is our pleasure to announce the dinner party will be held on Friday the 4th of March at the Food Palace. We will enjoy a 10−course Chinese banquet featuring many famous delicacies, such as Peking duck and braised pork belly. The first course will be served at 6:30 pm, so make sure to arrive before then.

Below are the results of the vote. We apologize to everyone who won't be able to attend and we hope that we will see you at our spring feast next year.

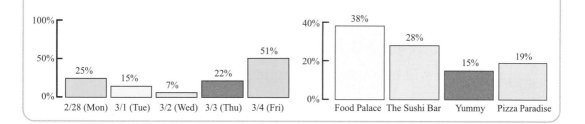

(   ) 2. According to the second letter, what are the date and restaurant of the banquet that the majority was in favor of?

(A) 2/28 (Mon), The Sushi Bar.   (B) 3/2 (Wed), Yummy.

(C) 3/3 (Thu), Pizza Paradise.   (D) 3/4 (Fri), Food Palace.

(　　) 3. Which of the following statement is true about the banquet?

    (A) Employees who attend the banquet can get red envelopes.

    (B) Employees who wish to attend should inform the Human Resources.

    (C) The banquet will contain 5 courses and start at half past six.

    (D) Besides Peking Duck and Braised Pork Belly, the restaurant also provides vegetarian dishes.

(　　) 4. Which of the following is true about the vote on the spring feast?

    (A) The smallest number of employees wish to eat sushi.

    (B) More than a quarter of the people pick Thursday.

    (D) Pizza and sushi are the two most popular choices.

    (C) Most employees do not wish to go to the banquet on Wednesday.

(　　) 5. What does the Human Resources mean by the last sentence of the second letter?

    (A) They feel sorry and promise to give a gift to those who can't attend.

    (B) They will soon plan another spring feast for those who can't attend.

    (C) The spring feast is an annual event. It's hoped those who can't attend are able to come next year.

    (D) There will be a vote on the spring feast next year. It's hoped all the employees are still willing to vote.

▶ Vocabulary & Phrases

1. **notify** [`notə‚faɪ] *vt.* 通知

    ＊We are notified that the flight has been cancelled.

2. **head count** [`hɛd‚kaʊnt] *n.* [C] 人數統計

    ＊The guide always does a head count before moving to the next place.

3. **apologize** [ə`pɑlə‚dʒaɪz] *vi.* 道歉

    ＊My friend apologized to me for being late.

4. **in advance** 事先

   ＊It will be much cheaper if you book the hotel in advance.

5. **banquet** [ˋbæŋkwɪt] *n.* [C] (正式的) 宴會

   ＊My friend and I were invited to the banquet.

6. **vegetarian** [ˌvɛdʒəˋtɛrɪən] *adj.* 素食的

   ＊I don't eat meat, so we decided to go to a vegetarian restaurant.

7. **annual** [ˋænjʊəl] *adj.* 每年一次的

   ＊Every employee is requested to attend the annual meeting for year-end discussion.

Words for Recognition

1. venue [ˋvɛnju] *n.* [C] 場所，舉行地點
2. RSVP 請回覆：法文 "répondez s'il vous plaît" 的縮寫，為「請回覆 (please respond)」的意思。
3. Chinese [tʃaɪˋniz] *adj.* 中國的
4. Japanese [ˌdʒæpəˋniz] *adj.* 日本的
5. American [əˋmɛrəkən] *adj.* 美國的
6. Italian [ɪˋtæljən] *adj.* 義大利的
7. sushi [ˋsuʃi] *n.* [U] 壽司
8. finalize [ˋfaɪnḷˌaɪz] *vt.* 定案
9. delicacy [ˋdɛləkəsɪ] *n.* [C] 佳餚
10. Peking duck 北京烤鴨
11. braised pork belly 紅燒肉

Pop Quiz

_____ 1. My neighbor n_____fied the police that her house had been broken into.

_____ 2. We need to reserve a table for two in a____e.

_____ 3. All the chefs are busy preparing for a royal b____t.

_____ 4. The company trip has become an a____l event in our company.

_____ 5. Kevin a____zed for his behavior and bad temper.

Unit 28

Telephone Messages

Below are two notes.

To:	*Roger*	From:	*Dave*	Taken By:	*Carol (#808)*

Extension: *#210*   Date: *2/2*   Time: *8:30*   (A.M.) / P.M.

1. *Dave's computer shut down automatically, and several files were missing. Please check his computer and help him recover those missing files.*

2. *Jimmy takes a day off today. Dave had sent the report Jimmy should give you today. Please let Dave know whether you have received the report.*

3. *Dave wants to reschedule a meeting with you. Instead of this Friday, can you meet him next Monday (2/9) morning at 9 or 10 o'clock? Because an extremely important client just informed Dave that he wanted to have a meeting with him this Friday. And Dave said he is genuinely sorry for that.*

Call Back Requested? (YES) / NO   Date/Time Completed   *2 / 2*

To:	*Dave*	From:	*Roger*	Taken By:	*Emma (#215)*

Extension: *#812*   Date: *2/2*   Time: *4:30*   A.M. / (P.M.)

1. *Roger will fix your computer tomorrow morning.*
   He supposed the hard disk in your computer is broken. He will have a bash at recovering your files. However, he cannot guarantee that all the files can be recovered.

2. *Roger said "Many thanks!" He had received the report. However, he has some questions about the report. He will call and ask Jimmy directly tomorrow.*

3. *Roger said, "Never mind." He is fine with 10 o'clock next Monday morning.*

Call Back Requested?   YES / (NO)   Date/Time Completed   *2 / 2*

(   ) 1. What are these two notes?

      (A) They are text messages.

      (B) They are electronic mail.

      (C) They are recorded voice messages.

      (D) They are interoffice phone messages.

(   ) 2. According to the notes, which of the following is true?

      (A) It is very likely that the employees work from nine to five.

      (B) Emma and Dave are likely to work in the same department.

      (C) Dave needs to call Roger back to discuss the problems.

      (D) Carol had called Dave back, but it was Emma who received the call.

(   ) 3. Which of the following problems is NOT mentioned in the notes?

      (A) Jimmy's report wasn't sent to Roger.

      (B) Dave's computer crashed and some of his files are missing.

      (C) Roger will call Jimmy to ask him questions about the report.

      (D) Roger might not be able to repair the files on Dave's computer.

(   ) 4. When will Dave and Roger have a meeting?

      (A) 10:00 P.M., Monday, February 2nd.

      (B) 10:00 A.M., Tuesday, February 3rd.

      (C) 10:00 P.M., Friday, February 6th.

      (D) 10:00 A.M., Monday, February 9th.

(   ) 5. What is most likely to be Roger's job?

      (A) Accountant.   (B) Secretary.

      (C) Computer engineer.   (D) Security officer.

→ Vocabulary & Phrases

1. **extension** [ɪk`stɛnʃən] *n.* [C] 電話分機

   *I dialed Justin's extension, but no one answered the phone.

2. **A.M.** [`e`ɛm] *abbr.* 上午

   *I usually get up at 6 A.M., or I will be late for school.

3. **P.M.** [`pi`ɛm] *abbr.* 下午

   *The dinner party will start at 7 P.M.

4. **shut down** (使) 停止運作

   *I bought a computer last week because my old one always shut down.

5. **day off** [`de‚ɔf] *n.* [C] 休假日 (pl. days off)

   *I went to visit my parents on my days off.

6. **genuinely** [`dʒɛnjʊɪnlɪ] *adv.* 真誠地

   *Peter is genuinely sorry for what he had done to me and keeps apologizing.

7. **have a bash (at sth.)** 嘗試做

   *I have never eaten a fried spider. I would like to have a bash at it when visiting Cambodia.

8. **guarantee** [‚gærən`ti] *vt.* 保證

   *The salesman guarantees that I can get a full refund.

9. **accountant** [ə`kaʊntənt] *n.* [C] 會計師

   *As an accountant, Cindy is good at numbers.

Words for Recognition

1. reschedule [ri`skɛdʒʊl] *vt.* 重新安排⋯的時間

2. hard disk [`hɑrd͵dɪsk] *n.* [C] 硬碟

Pop Quiz

_____ 1. My computer s_____ts down for it is overheating.

_____ 2. The supermarket g_____es their product with good quality and low price.

_____ 3. The man is g_____y interested in our new machine and wishes to buy one.

_____ 4. The company is hiring an a_____t for its accounting department.

_____ 5. May I have Linda's e_____n number, please?

Unit 29
Advertisement and Complaint Letter

Below are an advertisement and a complaint letter.

Fitness X
presents a new way to make enormous gains!
In less than a month!

Acceletron, the newest innovation in fitness technology, is a muscle-stimulator which can:

1. Build Your Muscles
2. Lose Your Weight
3. Improve Your Heart Function
4. Increase Your Overall Strength
5. Build up Your Physical Ability

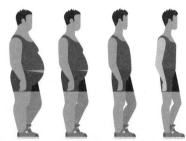

HOW IT WORKS

The Acceletron muscle-stimulator works by sending small electrical pulses throughout your body, causing your muscles to contract. These contractions are similar to the effect that exercise has on your body without causing the same injuries on it. This allows your muscles to grow faster and to labor for long hours.

Besides, it has been demonstrated that, on average, Acceletron can help you lose 10 pounds in a month.

To:	Fitness X
From:	John Harman
Subject:	Refund Request

Dear Fitness X,

I purchased your Acceletron muscle-stimulator two months ago and wanted to make a formal complaint about the product's quality.

Firstly, using the product is quite painful. The electric shocks often caused my whole body to move uncontrollably, which was very uncomfortable. Secondly, the product takes an extremely long time to charge. I often have to wait 12 hours before I can use it a second time. Lastly and most importantly, after a month of daily use I have seen no noticeable increase in my muscle mass or any loss of weight. It seems your product has no effect at all.

I am incredibly disappointed with your product and expect a full refund.

Sincerely,
John Harman

(   ) 1. What is the purpose of the advertisement?

    (A) To hire more employees.

    (B) To promote a new product.

    (C) To invite customers to its new branch.

    (D) To explain a new advanced technology.

(   ) 2. How does Acceletron muscle-stimulator help build muscles?

      (A) By stimulating the heartbeat.

      (B) By electrically shocking muscles.

      (C) By pulling the muscles to encourage growth.

      (D) By tricking people's brains into building muscles.

(   ) 3. Which of the following is NOT mentioned in John's letter?

      (A) The equipment is too expensive.

      (B) No desired effect has been achieved.

      (C) The electrical pulses were very unpleasant.

      (D) It takes too long to power up the equipment.

(   ) 4. How does John wish to be compensated?

      (A) A formal apology.

      (B) A discount for future purchases.

      (C) A new Acceletron muscle-stimulator.

      (D) A refund of the product he bought.

(   ) 5. The advertisement would most likely be found in a magazine about

      _____.

      (A) Fashion & Design.   (B) Fitness & Wellness.

      (C) Family & Education.   (D) Science & Environment.

► Vocabulary & Phrases

1. **overall** [ˌovɚ`ɔl] *adj.* 全部的，全面的

   ＊I was surprised that the overall cost of the program was one billion dollars.

2. **physical** [`fɪzɪkl̩] *adj.* 身體的

   ＊Taking exercise can increase your physical strength.

3. **pulse** [pʌls] *n.* [C] 脈衝

   ＊Scientists used sound pulses to measure the distance to the bottom of the cave.

4. **labor** [`lebɚ] *vi.* 勞動

＊My brother labored for many years as a fisherman.

5. **demonstrate** [`dɛmən‚stret] *vt.* 顯示

＊The research demonstrates that even young people can have Alzheimer's disease.

6. **on average** 平均上

＊On average, women do more housework than men.

7. **noticeable** [`notɪsəbḷ] *adj.* 顯著的

＊There is a noticeable improvement in the student's performance. They all get better grades now.

8. **refund** [`rɪfʌnd] *n.* [C] 退款

＊The customer took the product back to the store and asked for a refund.

9. **objective** [əb`dʒɛktɪv] *adj.* 客觀的

＊The journalists are supposed to be objective about what they write.

10. **stimulate** [`stɪmjə‚let] *vi / vt.* 刺激

＊The aim of the class is to stimulate the students to think creatively.

11. **compensate** [`kɑmpən‚set] *vt.* 賠償

＊The victims of the flood will be compensated by the government.

12. **apology** [ə`pɑlədʒɪ] *n.* [C] 道歉

＊I owned Tracy an apology for being rude to her.

Words for Recognition

1. stimulator [`stɪmjə‚letɚ] *n.* [C] 刺激器

Pop Quiz

_____ 1. Mark made an a____y for being late again.

_____ 2. The medicine has a n____e effect upon the patient. She gets better very fast.

_____ 3. It is hard for me to remain o____e all the time.

_____ 4. Exercising can bring both p____l and mental health benefits.

_____ 5. Despite some disadvantages, the o____l effect of the policy is positive.

Advertisement and Complaint Letter

Unit 30

The Red Kangaroo

Below is a passage with Joe's study note.

The red kangaroo is the largest of all the kangaroo species, weighing up to 90 kilograms and reaching a height of up to two meters.

Red kangaroos live on the dry open plains of Australia. Their normal hopping speed is around 25 km/h, but they can reach a top speed of around 70 km/h (and maintain a speed of 40 km/h for about two kilometers). They usually cover a distance of about 1.5 to 2 meters with each hop. However, when they move at top speed, their single leap may measure over 9 meters in length and up to 3 meters in height.

Red kangaroos live in most parts of the Australian Outback and are well adapted to the hot and dry conditions of the desert region. They can survive without drinking any water at all if there is enough fresh green grass for them to eat.

Adult male kangaroos are called bucks, adult females are known as does, and young kangaroos are joeys.

World record for
Men's long jump is 8.95 m!
Men's high jump is 2.45 m!

The "Outback" is a huge area covering most of Australia.

(   ) 1. What is this passage mainly about?

    (A) A brief introduction to the red kangaroos.

    (B) The species that live in the Australian Outback.

    (C) A comparison of kangaroos' physical abilities with those of humans.

    (D) The differences between the red kangaroos and other kangaroo species.

(   ) 2. According to the passage, which of the following is true about the red kangaroos?

    (A) Red kangaroos may grow to a height of 3 meters.

    (B) All red kangaroos weigh at least 90 kilograms.

    (C) Red kangaroos' natural habitat is shrinking due to climate change.

    (D) At full speed, a red kangaroo can jump farther than the men's long jump world record.

(   ) 3. How can red kangaroos survive in the hot and dry conditions of the desert region?

    (A) They are able to store water in their body.

    (B) They can get enough water by eating fresh grass.

    (C) They sleep for long periods to keep themselves cool.

    (D) They cover themselves in desert sands to avoid the heat.

(   ) 4. What notes have been written next to the passage for the red kangaroo?

    (A) The average age of the red kangaroo.

    (B) The mating habits of the red kangaroo.

    (C) The size of the population of the red kangaroo.

    (D) The names given to different genders and ages of the kangaroo.

(   ) 5. Which of the following can be inferred from the passage?

       (A) Most of the land in the Australian Outback is covered by desert.

       (B) At top speed, the red kangaroo can travel the Outback within one day.

       (C) Instead of drinking water, the red kangaroo prefers to have fresh grass.

       (D) The poor habitation will endanger the red kangaroo in the near future.

澳洲常見動物

袋獾 tasmanian devil

袋熊 wombat

針鼴 echidna

笑翠鳥 kookaburra

袋鼠 kangaroo

無尾熊 koala

鴨嘴獸 platypus

傘蜥蜴 frill-necked lizard

鴯鶓 emu

➤ Vocabulary & Phrases

1. **species** [`spiʃɪz] *n. pl.* (生物分類) 種

   ＊Lions and tigers are different species.

2. **measure** [`mɛʒɚ] *vt.* 測量

   ＊Students are being measured for new uniforms.

3. **adapt** [ə`dæpt] *vi. / vt.* (使) 適應

   ＊Barton has difficulty in adapting quickly to the new surroundings.

4. **habitat** [`hæbə͵tæt] *n.* [C] 棲地

   ＊The tourists caused pollution to the wildlife habitat by throwing garbage around.

5. **gender** [`dʒɛndɚ] *n.* [C] [U] 性別

   ＊Gender stereotypes about what men and women should be like still exist.

➤ Words for Recognition

1. Australia 澳洲：位於大洋洲，是世界上唯一一個國土覆蓋整個大陸的國家。境內有多樣的自然景觀和珍貴動植物物種。

2. The Australian Outback 澳洲內陸：氣候乾燥，多為草原和荒漠。

➤ Pop Quiz

_____ 1. Because of environmental pollution, hundreds of s_____s have disappeared in the past century.

_____ 2. The refugees found it hard to a____t to the local culture.

_____ 3. The customer is m____ring the bed size for sheets.

_____ 4. The doctor has found out the g____r of the unborn baby through the test.

_____ 5. Because of global warming, polar bears are losing their natural h____ts.

Unit 31
Sky Lanterns: Not Just Harmless Fun

Sky lanterns are small paper hot air balloons that are used in traditional festivals across Asia. In China and Taiwan, their usage is central to the Spring Lantern Festival, in which thousands of sky lanterns are lighted and float together across the night sky. However, the practice of lighting sky lanterns is under examination due to a danger to wildlife and the possibility of causing fires.

Despite its cultural significance, experts have warned fallen sky lanterns are a fire hazard. In one case, a sky lantern was the cause of a fire at a plastic factory in Smethwick, England. The lantern landed on the factory, **igniting** materials stored there and causing a disastrous fire. Over 200 firefighters were called to the scene to put out the fire.

Fires aren't the only problems sky lanterns can cause. They can also harm wildlife, too. Cattle died after the metal wires of a lantern ended up in their feed and caused them internal bleeding. A young horse had to be put down after severely injuring its legs when it was startled by a fallen lantern.

Events like these have motivated calls to ban the sale and use of sky lanterns entirely. Now, sky lanterns are illegal in Germany and Austria, and many states in Australia have banned the sale of sky lanterns due to the high risk of bush fires there. Sky lanterns may seem harmless enough, but they have the potential to cause devastating fires and pose a serious threat to wildlife. Therefore, we must take action to deal with the problem before it is too late.

生
態
保
育

(   ) 1. What is the main idea of this passage?

    (A) Sky lanterns are a must in the Spring Lantern Festival.

    (B) Firefighters successfully put out a fire caused by sky lanterns.

    (C) Sky lanterns are threatening the environment as well as animals.

    (D) Sky lanterns' cultural meaning is far more important than its potential danger.

(   ) 2. What does "**igniting**" in the second paragraph most likely refer to?

    (A) Covering.   (B) Lighting.

    (C) Making up.   (D) Knocking over.

(   ) 3. Why have some states of Australia banned the sale of sky lanterns?

    (A) Sky lanterns kill their cattle.

    (B) Sky lanterns tend to cause fire.

    (C) Sky lanterns land on their factories.

    (D) Sky lanterns have left their horses injured.

(   ) 4. What is the author's attitude toward sky lanterns?

    (A) Neutral.   (B) Indifferent.

    (C) For it.   (D) Against it.

(   ) 5. What is most likely to be discussed in the next paragraph?

    (A) The approach to a world free of sky lanterns.

    (B) A new technology that can be applied to sky lanterns.

    (C) More examples of the damage caused by fallen sky lanterns.

    (D) Debates about whether people should preserve wildlife or the environment.

➤ Vocabulary & Phrases

1. **usage** [`jusɪdʒ] *n.* [U] 使用

   ＊Public transportation can reduce the usage of cars and motorcycles.

2. **despite** [dɪ`spaɪt] *prep.* 儘管，不顧

   ＊John didn't get any award despite all his efforts to finish the project.

3. **significance** [sɪg`nɪfəkəns] *n.* [U] 重要；意義

   ＊The new policy has great significance for the social equality.

4. **hazard** [`hæzɚd] *n.* [C] 危險

   ＊Exposed electrical wires are fire hazards.

5. **disastrous** [dɪz`æstrəs] *adj.* 災禍的，不幸的

   ＊The bad decision brought the company a disastrous result.

6. **severely** [sə`vɪrlɪ] *adv.* 嚴重地

   ＊The man who abused stray dogs has been severely criticized.

7. **startle** [`stɑrtl̩] *vt.* 使驚嚇

   ＊The loud noise of firecrackers startled the little baby.

8. **motivate** [`motəˌvet] *vt.* 引起動機

   ＊People were motivated to donate to the charity.

9. **ban** [bæn] *vt.* 明令禁止

   ＊Because of drunk driving, the man was banned from driving.

10. **mercy** [`mɝsɪ] *n.* [U] 慈悲

    ＊The army showed no mercy to the enemy.

生態保育

Words for Recognition

1. Asia 亞洲：全球七大洲中面積最大，人口最多的一個洲。絕大部分土地位於東半球和北半球

2. Smethwick 斯梅西克：位於英國的一座城市。

3. ignite [ig`naɪt] *vi. / vt.* 點燃

4. put down 殺死 (衰老或有傷病的動物以免除其痛苦)

5. Germany 德國：位於歐洲，是歐盟中人口最多的國家，其工業和科技技術位居世界前列。

6. Austria 奧地利：位於歐洲中部的國家。首都為音樂之都—維也納。

7. devastating [`dɛvəs,tetɪŋ] *adj.* 毀滅性的

Pop Quiz

_____ 1. The discovery of the new evidence has great s_____e to the unsolved case.

_____ 2. The book was b_____ned in the country during the Cold War.

_____ 3. The soldier was s_____y injured in the war, he lost both his legs.

_____ 4. The painter was m_____ted to create the painting of the landscape.

_____ 5. D_____e its discount, many people still refused to buy the product.

Green Industry Seminar Agenda

Earth Watch's Annual Green Industry Seminar

A series of talks to be held on Mon. 9/18, 09:00–16:00

at Grand Plaza Hotel, Conference Hall 2

Earth Watch aims to help governments and organizations limit their environmental impact by encouraging the use of **green options** for their infrastructure. Attendees will learn about the various eco-friendly equipment and management practices in fields relating to environmental protection.

AGENDA

Time	Conference Room	Topic and Speaker
09:00–09:30	A	***Opening***—Joseph Yamamoto a. Introduction b. Overview of the agenda and objectives
09:30–10:40	A	***Water and Wastewater***—Elizabeth Morin a. Waste Treatment and Recycling Equipment b. Water Treatment c. Pure Water Treatment
10:40–11:00	**Coffee Break** (Light refreshments are available in the hallway.)	
11:00–12:00	A	***Sewage Sludge Treatment and Recycling***—Carl Rosin
	B	***Air Pollution Prevention***—Martin Schultz
12:00–13:30	**Lunch Break**	
13:30–14:40	A	***Waste Management and Recycling***—David Hobart
	B	***Organic Products***—Ellen Hales
14:40–15:00	**Coffee Break** (Light refreshments are available in the hallway.)	
15:00–16:00	A	***Wrap up***—Joseph Yamamoto a. Q & A b. Lottery c. Announcement of the next seminar

生
態
保
育

(   ) 1. What is the main purpose of the seminar?

       (A) To enforce the laws on pollution control.

       (B) To encourage the companies to grow more plants.

       (C) To advise on environmentally friendly solutions.

       (D) To help organizations find economical equipment.

(   ) 2. Which of the following is closest in meaning to "**green options**" in the first paragraph?

       (A) The infrastructure would be painted in green.

       (B) The infrastructure can help protect the environment.

       (C) Governments must build a park as green infrastructure.

       (D) People would be green with envy if you were one of the attendees.

(   ) 3. How many breaks do attendees get to relax during the seminar?

       (A) 1.   (B) 2.   (C) 3.   (D) 4.

(   ) 4. Which of the following does NOT happen at the end of the seminar?

       (A) Attendees can raise questions.

       (B) The host will introduce the next seminar.

       (C) Attendees have a chance to win something.

       (D) Free gifts will be given out to all the attendees.

(   ) 5. Mr. Wang is interested in natural food. Which of the following sessions should he attend?

       (A) 11:00−12:00, Conference Room A.

       (B) 11:00−12:00, Conference Room B.

       (C) 13:30−14:40, Conference Room A.

       (D) 13:30−14:40, Conference Room B.

Unit 32

Vocabulary & Phrases

1. **seminar** [ˋsɛmə͵nɑr] *n.* [C] 研討會

   ＊Workers at the company were asked to attend the seminar on sales.

2. **agenda** [əˋdʒɛndə] *n.* [C] (會議) 議程

   ＊The first item on the agenda is the training budget.

3. **option** [ˋɑpʃən] *n.* [C] 選擇

   ＊The customers have various options for food in the restaurant.

4. **objective** [əbˋdʒɛktɪv] *n.* [C] 目標

   ＊The main objective of the policy is to reduce crime.

5. **recycle** [riˋsaɪkl̩] *vi. / vt.* 回收

   ＊In order to protect the environment, the government encourages people to recycle paper and bottles.

6. **refreshments** [rɪˋfrɛʃmənts] *n. pl.* 茶點

   ＊The host will provide refreshments during the break.

7. **wrap up** 圓滿完成，順利結束 (會議)

   ＊We will wrap up the meeting this afternoon.

8. **pollution** [pəˋluʃən] *n.* [U] 污染

   ＊Air pollution from the factory has bad influence on the local people's health.

9. **organic** [ɔrˋgænɪk] *adj.* 有機的

   ＊Organic products are generally more expensive than regular products.

10. **enforce** [ɪnˋfors] *vt.* 實行

    ＊People are asking the government to enforce tougher laws on drunk driving.

11. **economical** [͵ikəˋnɑmɪkl̩] *adj.* 節約的，節儉的

    ＊Electric cars are more economical than gas-powered cars.

Words for Recognition

1. infrastructure [ˋɪnfrəˌstrʌktʃɚ] *n.* [C] 基礎建設
2. attendee [əˋtɛndi] *n.* [C] 出席者，參加者
3. sewage [ˋsjuɪdʒ] *n.* [U] 汙水
4. sludge [slʌdʒ] *n.* [U] 爛泥，淤泥

Pop Quiz

_____ 1. Many political commentators said the new policy would be hard to e____ e.

_____ 2. Most people believe o____ c food is good for health.

_____ 3. You should follow the action plan to achieve your o____ e.

_____ 4. The boy r____ led the bottle and made it into a vase.

_____ 5. The factory was fined for causing water p____ n.

Unit 33

The Big Coastal Cleanup

Below are a leaflet and a piece of news.

Let's Clean the Beach

The Westfield Beach Association (WBA) is holding a coastal cleanup event on June 8th. We're hoping to make this our biggest cleanup ever, so bring a couple of friends or family members—young or old, it doesn't matter!

This year, Charlie's Bagel Café is sponsoring our coastal cleanup and will provide us with coffee and bagels to keep us going. Bring your own reusable cups and plates.

Why not enter our cleanup contest? Teams of four will compete to see which one can collect the most trash. The winners will get a fun mystery prize! Help us spread the word about the cleanup. See you soon!

You should wear and prepare

- Wide Brim Hat
- Scarf
- Linen Gloves
- Arm Sleeve
- Short Sleeve T-Shirts
- Sneakers
- Pants / Shorts with Leggings
- Backpack / Drawstring
- Sport Water Bottle

We will provide

- Pen
- Scale
- Tongs
- Record Sheet
- Clipboard
- Sack

(Westfield Star) — Dozens of volunteers gathered at Westfield Beach yesterday to participate in an annual beach cleanup. Kate Evans, the Director of the Westfield Beach Association, estimates that nearly half a ton of garbage was collected. "There was actually a lot less trash than last year, which we're pleased about. Our long-term goal is to educate people not to leave their garbage at the beach in the first place. **The message** seems to be getting through," said Evans. The weather was quite cool and windy, but over 100 people still turned up for the event. "We're delighted that so many people showed up. We had whole families down there, from grandmas to little kids, picking up trash and having a great time. It was amazing!" added Evans.

( ) 1. What is the purpose of the leaflet?

　　(A) To encourage people to attend an event.

　　(B) To emphasize the importance of family.

　　(C) To invite companies to sponsor the event.

　　(D) To raise public awareness of environmental protection.

( ) 2. According to the leaflet, which of the following were coastal cleanup volunteers required to bring with them?

　　(A) Snacks.　　　　　　　　　(B) Gloves.

　　(C) Trash bags.　　　　　　　(D) Record sheets.

( ) 3. Why were the volunteers asked to bring reusable cups and plates?

　　(A) They would get free food and drinks.

　　(B) They could collect more trash in this way.

　　(C) They were going to recycle the cups and plates.

　　(D) They needed the cups and plates to enter a contest.

Unit 33

(   ) 4. What does "**The message**" in the news refer to?

    (A) The cleanup is an amazing event.

    (B) People are welcome to join the cleanup.

    (C) People shouldn't leave trash on the beach.

    (D) Families can have a great time picking up trash.

(   ) 5. Which of the following is true about this year's coastal cleanup?

    (A) Children were not allowed to join the event.

    (B) Less than one hundred people joined the event.

    (C) Volunteers were provided with refreshments.

    (D) Volunteers were asked to pay an entrance fee.

➤ Vocabulary & Phrases

1. **association** [ə͵sosɪˋeʃən] *n.* [C] 協會

   ∗Amy has worked for the association for ten years.

2. **sponsor** [ˋspɑnsɚ] *vt.* 贊助

   ∗The basketball team is sponsored by a famous company.

3. **keep going** (在身處困境或遭難時) 盡力維持下去，堅持活下去

   ∗Sometimes it is hard to keep going, but we still stick to our goal.

4. **contest** [ˋkɑntɛst] *n.* [C] 比賽

   ∗Sammy entered the singing contest and won first prize.

5. **sneaker** [ˋsnikɚ] *n.* [C] 運動鞋

   ∗You had better wear sneakers while playing basketball, or you might sprain your ankle.

6. **backpack** [ˋbæk͵pæk] *n.* [C] 背包

   ∗I bought my new backpack in the sales.

7. **volunteer** [͵vɑlənˋtɪr] *n.* [C] 志工

   ∗School is calling for volunteers to receive the foreign students.

生
態
保
育

8. **estimate** [`ɛstəmet] *vt.* 估計

   ＊Tom estimates that he will need eight million dollars to buy a house.

9. **in the first place** 最初，原本

   ＊Michele said she should listen to me in the first place

10. **turn up** 到達，突然出現

    ＊My best friend turned up at my farewell party at the last moment.

11. **delighted** [dɪ`laɪtɪd] *adj.* 高興的

    ＊The man was delighted at the news of the promotion.

12. **supervise** [`supɚˌvaɪz] *vi. / vt.* 監督，管理

    ＊Vivian's job is to supervise the workers to make sure they work hard.

Words for Recognition

1. coastal [kostḷ] *adj.* 沿岸的
2. cleanup [`klinˌʌp] *n.* [C][U] 清潔，整頓
3. bagel [`begəl] *n.* 貝果
4. brim [brɪm] *n.* [C] 帽簷
5. leggings [`lɛgɪŋz] *n. pl.* 內搭褲
6. drawstring bag [`drɔˌstrɪŋˌbæg] *n.* [C] 束口袋
7. tongs [tɔŋz] *n. pl.* 夾子

Pop Quiz

_____ 1. I was d____d to meet my old classmates after so many years.

_____ 2. It is e____ted that the ruined temple will take ten years to rebuild.

_____ 3. My mother has worked as a v____r in the hospital for more than fifteen years.

_____ 4. The student represents her school in the English speech c____t.

_____ 5. The scientific research is s____red by the government.

Unit 34

Help Us Save Our Oceans

Below are two letters.

✉		— ☐ ✕
To:	Department of Marine Biology	
From:	Save Our Oceans	
Subject:	Invite You to Our Speech on the Depletion of Fish Stocks	

Dear Department of Marine Biology,

You are sincerely invited to attend a series of speeches about the gradual depletion of fish stocks in our oceans due to overfishing.

Over the course of the event, we aim to address the problem of overfishing and present possible solutions to **this growing concern**. It is our hope that your presence at our seminar will in some way help the fight to safeguard our precious oceans and make the future better for everyone.

Our first speaker is David Hoffman, a professional in the field of marine ecosystem management, who will elaborate on the changes in our fish populations that have occurred since the 1980s. Our second-day speaker will be Jill Abernathy, who will be talking about the problems with fishing regulations and their enforcement. Our third and final speaker is George Bogart, the head of the River and Ocean Protection Commission. He will be giving a talk on what needs to be done in order to ensure sustainable fishing in the future.

Time and Date: 9:00–12:00, 3/12–3/14   Location: Red Dragon Hotel, Hall 4
Ticket Price: Single ticket   NT$ 150 (Choose any one of the speeches.)
            Dual package   NT$ 250 (Choose any two of the speeches.)
            Full package   NT$ 300 (Attend entire three speeches.)

Reserve online at www.saveouroceans.com/eventbookings
(All the attendees should make a reservation in advance)

If there is any question, please let us know.

With anticipation,
Save Our Oceans

Call: (02)1234–5678

生態保育

✉			− □ ×
To:	Save Our Oceans		
From:	Cynthia		
Subject:	Inquiry about Single Tickets		

Dear Save Our Oceans,

We are really interested in the seminar and like to place an order for the tickets. A rough estimate of the single tickets we need is between 100 and 120. Please let us know how many seats you can offer. Besides, we would like to know if you can grant us a special discount.

I look forward to hearing from you.

Sincerely,
Cynthia
Assistant, Department of Marine Biology

(   ) 1. According to the first email, what are the speeches mainly about?

    (A) Biology.   (B) Overfishing.

    (C) Marine life.   (D) Fishing regulations.

(   ) 2. What is the purpose of the second email?

    (A) To ask for a refund.   (B) To make a complaint.

    (C) To give advice on fishing.   (D) To request more information.

(   ) 3. What does "**this growing concern**" in the first email refer to?

    (A) The reduction in fish stocks.

    (B) Audiences' absence from the speeches.

    (C) Marine pollution caused by fishing boats.

    (D) The problem of reforming fishing regulations.

Unit 34

(   ) 4. Which of the following statement is NOT true about the event?

      (A) The event lasts for three days.

      (B) People can buy a ticket on the spot.

      (C) It is hosted by an environmental organization.

      (D) The speeches all start from 9:00 and end at noon.

(   ) 5. Which of the following can be inferred from the second email?

      (A) Cynthia rejects to attend the seminar.

      (B) Cynthia demands to get a reply immediately.

      (C) Cynthia wishes to buy the tickets at a lower price.

      (D) Cynthia is sure that there are enough seats for 100 people.

➤ Vocabulary & Phrases

1. **marine** [mə`rin] *adj.* 海的，海生的

   ＊The effects of oil pollution on marine life are harmful.

2. **biology** [baɪ`alədʒɪ] *n.* [U] 生物學

   ＊Peter has a degree in biology.

3. **stock** [stɑk] *n.* [C] 供應物

   ＊Fish stocks are under threat due to overfishing.

4. **elaborate** [ɪ`læbə‚ret] *vi. / vt.* 詳盡說明

   ＊The politician is elaborating his political views on TV.

5. **regulation** [‚rɛgjə`leʃən] *n.* [C] 規則

   ＊Many new regulations on imports were put to protect the domestic industry.

6. **enforcement** [ɪn`forsmənt] *n.* [C][U] 執行；強迫

   ＊People are calling for tighter enforcement of the laws on corruption.

7. **commission** [kə`mɪʃən] *n.* [C] (官方) 委員會

   ＊The school set up a commission on gender equality.

8. **ensure** [ɪn`ʃʊr] *vt.* 確保

   ＊Please ensure that all the errors have been fixed.

生態保育

9. **dual** [`djuəl] *adj.* 雙重的

   ＊My nephew has dual Taiwanese and American nationality.

10. **scan** [skæn] *vi.* / *vt.* 掃描

    ＊The clerk scanned the bar code on the products for their prices.

11. **reservation** [ˌrɛzɚ`veʃən] *n.* [C] 預訂

    ＊I'll make a reservation at the café for 3 P.M. this afternoon.

12. **anticipation** [ænˌtɪsə`peʃən] *n.* [U] 期望

    ＊We are full of anticipation and can't wait to go on the graduation trip.

13. **inquiry** [ɪn`kwaɪrɪ] *n.* 詢問

    ＊I've been making inquiries about the concert tickets for the date and time.

14. **email** [`imel] *n.* [C][U] 電子郵件

    ＊Bob said he didn't receive the email from me.

15. **estimate** [`ɛstəmɪt] *n.* [C] 估算

    ＊An estimate of the number of the flood victims has been over 100 people.

16. **grant** [grænt] *vt.* 同意，准予

    ＊The sick student is granted to hand in his homework a week later.

➤ Words for Recognition

1. depletion [dɪ`pliʃən] *n.* [U] 減少，耗損
2. ecosystem [`ikoˌsɪstəm] *n.* [C] 生態系統
3. sustainable [sə`stenəbl̩] *adj.* 永續的

➤ Pop Quiz

_____ 1. Because of terrorist attacks, the immigration r_____ns have become tighter.

_____ 2. The student went on to e_____e her study plan.

_____ 3. Lisa is g_____ted to stay in this country for one year.

_____ 4. M_____e life is under threat due to climate change.

_____ 5. The police promise that they will do anything to e_____e the hostage's safety.

Unit 34

Unit 35
A Billboard That Makes Water from Thin Air

What could be better than a nice glass of cool clean drinking water? How about a nice glass of cool clean drinking water that was made by a billboard? **Yes, you read that correctly.**

In Lima, Peru, a new kind of billboard has been designed that quite literally extracts water from thin air. Sandwiched between the front and the back of the billboard is a complex system of high-tech filters.

In the first stage, an air filter removes particles from the air as the wind blows through the billboard. This air is then cooled by a series of cold pipes, which cause all the water in the air to turn into large drops, in the same way that rain is formed. This water then passes through a carbon filter and collected in a cold tank. Next, gravity carries the water down a pipe to a faucet near the ground.

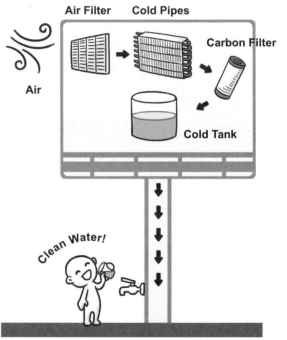

The billboard collects more than 100 liters a day, providing much-needed drinking water in a city that receives less than half an inch of rainfall per year. The lack of rain can be explained by the area's unique geography. To the west of Lima lies the Pacific Ocean, which means the air is very humid. However, to the north of the city lies one of the driest deserts on earth. Over 1.2 million people in Lima lack running water, so the billboard offers hope that their dream of having access to clean, cheap drinking water may be just around the corner.

(   ) 1. What is the author's attitude toward the high-tech billboard?

    (A) Confident.   (B) Indifferent.   (C) Hostile.   (D) Suspicious.

(   ) 2. Why does the author say, "**Yes, you read that correctly**" in the first paragraph?

    (A) To make fun of the reader's poor reading skills.

    (B) To educate the reader about a basic fact about billboards.

    (C) To encourage people to question everything they read.

    (D) To emphasize the fact that a billboard can make drinking water.

(   ) 3. According to the passage, what is the original source of the water that the billboard collects from?

    (A) The clouds.   (B) The inland rivers.

    (C) The humid air.   (D) The Atlantic Ocean.

(   ) 4. What happens to the water in the final stage before it is stored in the cold tank?

    (A) Its temperature is lowered.

    (B) It goes through a carbon filter.

    (C) It is mixed with pure rainwater.

    (D) It is broken down into tiny particles.

(   ) 5. What does the author mean by the last sentence of the passage?

    (A) People in Lima might soon have access to cheap drinking water.

    (B) We should never underestimate the power of creative thinking.

    (C) More high-tech billboards are built, but greater investment is needed.

    (D) The climate is changing rapidly so we must do something before it's too late.

Unit 35

Vocabulary & Phrases

1. **literally** [ˋlɪtərəlɪ] *adv.* 照字義地

   ＊"Crocodile tears" doesn't literally mean a crocodile cries. It means that someone shows insincere sympathy.

2. **extract** [ɪkˋstrækt] *vt.* 萃取

   ＊It is said that oil extracted from olives is good for health.

3. **filter** [ˋfɪltɚ] *n.* [C] 過濾器

   ＊I will need an air filter to combat air pollution.

4. **particle** [ˋpɑrtɪkl̩] *n.* [C] 微粒，顆粒

   ＊People wear surgical masks to protect themselves from dust particles in the air.

5. **carbon** [ˋkɑrbən] *n.* [U] 碳

   ＊Carbon fiber has been used in aircrafts because of its low weight and high strength.

6. **gravity** [ˋgrævətɪ] *n.* [U] 地心引力

   ＊Water flows downwards due to gravity.

7. **ground** [graʊnd] *n.* [U] 地面

   ＊We set up our tent on the ground when camping.

8. **liter** [ˋlitɚ] *n.* [C] 公升

   ＊The doctor suggests drinking two liters of water every day.

9. **rainfall** [ˋrenˏfɔl] *n.* [U] 降雨量

   ＊The government has reminded the public to conserve water because rainfall in this month is below the average.

10. **access** [ˋæksɛs] *n.* [U] (使用到的) 機會

    ＊Only club members have access to the new equipment.

11. **hostile** [ˋhɑstl̩] *adj.* 懷敵意的

    ＊Although Michael has a hostile look, he is actually soft-hearted.

12. **inland** [ˋɪnlənd] *adj.* 內陸的

    ＊The Caspian sea is the largest inland sea in the world.

13. **underestimate** [ˌʌndɚˈɛstəˌmet] *vi. / vt.* 低估

 ＊We underestimated the time we would need to get to the airport and missed our plane.

14. **investment** [ɪnˈvɛstmənt] *n.* [C][U] 投資

 ＊This hospital has made a large investment in medical technology.

Words for Recognition

1. billboard [ˈbɪlˌbord] *n.* [C] 大型廣告看板

2. Lima 利馬：秘魯首都。

3. Peru 秘魯：位於南美洲西部。安地斯山脈縱貫國土南北，西部沿海為乾旱平原，東部為亞馬遜盆地。境內不同族群的人民造就多元的文化。

4. the Pacific Ocean 太平洋：地球面積最大的洋。西面為亞洲、大洋洲，東面為美洲。

5. the Atlantic Ocean 大西洋：世界第二大洋。西面為南美洲、北美洲，東面為歐洲、非洲。

Pop Quiz

_____ 1. "A yellow dog" doesn't l____y mean a dog with yellow fur. It means a cowardly person.

_____ 2. Research has shown that c____n dioxide is one of the gases that cause global warming.

_____ 3. My friend's dog is h____e to me and keeps barking at me.

_____ 4. Think twice before making decisions. Any i____t has a potential risk to lose money.

_____ 5. The company has u____ed the profit of the project and regrets not having invested it.

Unit 35

Unit 36
Pressing Safety Concern in Stillwater Valley

The Ministry of Economic Affairs' Central Geological Survey has released surprising findings. The findings show that 30% of the lands in Stillwater Valley are at risk of soil liquefaction.

Soil liquefaction is the process whereby wet soil can behave like a liquid when a sudden force is applied to it, such as during an earthquake. Usually when the soil is squeezed by the weight of buildings, the pressure will cause underground water to flow to the surface. However, if there are strong, sudden or repeated movements in the earth, the water does not have time to flow, and the soil grains separate. This separation causes the soil to behave like a liquid, making the ground very unstable.

The consequences of soil liquefaction in urban areas range from minor damage to road and infrastructure to the collapse of large buildings. Therefore, it is a high-priority issue for the government to address.

Stillwater Valley is particularly vulnerable to soil liquefaction because the soil has been saturated with river water. The soil is also especially fine-grained, which further increases the likelihood of soil liquefaction. This is causing some safety problems for the people living in these high-risk zones.

Even so the residential areas in the east are relatively safe; the biggest concern is the northern industrial district of Burswood, which is at the most risk. The coal power plant there provides the primary source of power for the entire city, so when faced with soil liquefaction, the city is at a very real risk of a power failure that could last for weeks or even months.

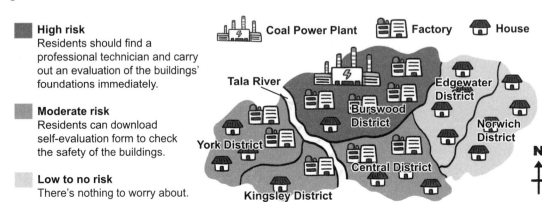

High risk
Residents should find a professional technician and carry out an evaluation of the buildings' foundations immediately.

Moderate risk
Residents can download self-evaluation form to check the safety of the buildings.

Low to no risk
There's nothing to worry about.

Coal Power Plant   Factory   House

Tala River
Burswood District
Edgewater District
Norwich District
York District
Central District
Kingsley District

N

(　　) 1. What does soil liquefaction mean?

    (A) Soil turns into mud after it is mixed with water and snow.

    (B) Soil is strengthened to a great extent due to the weight of buildings.

    (C) Most of the large and heavy buildings tend to collapse during an earthquake.

    (D) Underground water can't flow to the surface of the ground, making the ground behave like a liquid.

(　　) 2. Why is soil liquefaction a serious threat to Stillwater Valley?

    (A) It has lots of industrial areas.

    (B) Its buildings were poorly built.

    (C) It is in the geologically sensitive area.

    (D) The government didn't do anything actively.

(　　) 3. Which of the following districts is free from the risk brought by soil liquefaction?

    (A) York District.   (B) Central District.

    (C) Norwich District.   (D) Burswood District.

(　　) 4. What can we learn from the map?

    (A) Tala river goes through York District and Central District.

    (B) Most of the residents live in York District and Kingsley District.

    (C) Factories are mainly located in Edgewater District and Central District.

    (D) Residents in Burswood District don't have to worry about the soil liquefaction.

Pressing Safety Concern in Stillwater Valley

(   ) 5. What can we infer from the passage?

      (A) The city might be flooded when an earthquake hits.

      (B) People in high-risk areas must move to safer areas immediately.

      (C) People in medium-risk areas have nothing to worry about.

      (D) There might be a power failure in the city when an earthquake hits.

▶ Vocabulary & Phrases

1. **ministry** [`mɪnɪstrɪ] *n.* [C] (政府的) 部

   ＊Ministry of Foreign Affairs deals with international relationship between our nation and other countries.

2. **economic** [ˌikə`nɑmɪk] *adj.* 經濟的

   ＊The economic policy attempts to attract more foreign investments.

3. **consequence** [`kɑnsəˌkwɛns] *n.* [C] 結果

   ＊Eric is now suffering the consequences of eating too much ice cream.

4. **vulnerable** [`vʌlnərəbḷ] *adj.* 易受傷害的

   ＊Infants and children are vulnerable to the flu.

5. **likelihood** [`laɪklɪˌhʊd] *n.* [U] 可能，可能性

   ＊Look at the dark cloud; in all likelihood it will rain tonight.

6. **residential** [ˌrɛzə`dɛnʃəl] *adj.* 居住的，住宅的

   ＊Christine will move to a quiet residential area next month.

7. **district** [`dɪstrɪkt] *n.* [C] (行政) 區

   ＊Many historic buildings are located in the West Central District in Tainan.

8. **evaluation** [ɪˌvæljʊ`eʃən] *n.* [C] 評價，評估

   ＊The government will make an evaluation of the public construction.

9. **foundation** [faʊn`deʃən] *n.* [C] 地基

   ＊The workers finished laying the foundations of the new building.

10. **moderate** [`mɑdərɪt] *adj.* 中等的

   ＊Statistics show that there is a moderate inflation, so food price will increase a bit in the near future.

生態保育

11. **download** [ˋdaʊnˌlod] *vt.* 下載 (電腦上的資料)

＊People can download the e-books and read them on their smartphones.

12. **collapse** [kəˋlæps] *n.* [U] 倒塌 ｜ *vi.* 倒塌

＊To keep the temple from collapse, the workers are repairing the walls.

＊The building collapsed in the earthquake, and many people were trapped in broken bricks.

Words for Recognition

1. pressing [ˋprɛsɪŋ] *adj.* 緊迫的，迫切的

2. geological [ˌdʒɪəˋladʒɪkl] *adj.* 地質的

   geologically [ˌdʒɪəˋladʒɪklɪ] *adv.* 地質地

3. soil liquefaction 土壤液化：指土壤因地震等外力擠壓，使深層土壤的水份被擠壓到表層，而讓土讓呈現如液態的狀況。

4. whereby [hwɛrˋbaɪ] *adv.* 由於，從而

5. saturate [ˋsætʃəˌret] *vt.* 使濕透，飽含

6. fine-grained [ˋfaɪnˌgrend] *adj.* 質地細的

Pop Quiz

_____ 1. There is every l_____d that it will rain tomorrow.

_____ 2. The new product brought the company great e_____c success.

_____ 3. The bridge c_____ed during the flood, so we need to take a boat.

_____ 4. Frank now has to take the c_____es of his bad behavior.

_____ 5. Fry the eggs over a m_____e heat for one minute.

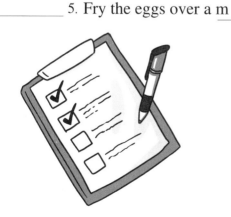

打好英文文法基礎
讓你大考輕鬆得分

Basic English Grammar Guide
英文文法入門指引

呂香瑩／著

本書特色：

1. 本書為針對英文初學者所苦惱的文法而設計。
2. 內容包括五大基礎句型、各種詞性與其用法，各種句型與其延伸應用
3. 多種文法透過表格整理，化繁為簡，以利綜合比較、釐清觀念。
4. 多種迷你單元，一眼記住文法關鍵。利用簡單圖示比較掌握複雜的概念。
5. 團訂附贈隨堂評量卷。

Reading Power 系列

★ 多益英語測驗/全民英檢初/中級適用
★ 學科能力測驗/指定科目考試/統一入學測驗適用

Intermediate

英閱百匯

解析本

Let's Read Real-World English!

車昀庭　　　　審閱
蘇文賢　　　　審訂
三民英語編輯小組　彙編

三民書局

Contents

綠 島

◆ 機場：從臺東飛綠島每天有三個班次。然而，冬天常因天候不佳而取消班機。夏季月份則必須提早數週預定航班。來往綠島的飛機是 19 人座，飛行時間為 15 分鐘。

◆ 綠島人權文化園區：這個以前關政治犯的監獄現在開放遊客參觀。遊客可以造訪博物館和展覽館，了解歷史。

◆ 觀音洞：觀音洞由地下伏流經過而形成。洞內有個天然形似憐憫眾生的女神觀音的石筍。傳說以前有漁民在海上迷航，受到神祕火球的指引返回岸邊，找到觀音石筍。漁民於是在洞內設置祭壇，以膜拜觀音。

◆ 登山健行步道：島上有兩條短的古步道。從島的東側開始走，一路向上到阿眉山頂。那裡風光明媚，而且如果運氣好的話，還能看到梅花鹿。

◆ 朝日溫泉：在大海旁邊泡溫泉，同時看日出。

◆ 大白沙：大白沙是知名潛水區，適合首次嘗試浮潛的觀光客和認真的水肺潛水人。這裡也是觀賞日落的人氣景點。

(B) 1. 根據本文，下列關於飛往綠島的班次，何者正確？
　　　　(A) 夏季時，人們可於現場得到機票。
　　　　(B) 每天排有三個航班。
　　　　(C) 夏季每天有一個航班。
　　　　(D) 有臺中到綠島的班機。

(C) 2. 觀音洞有何特別之處？
　　　　(A) 一位出名漁夫最後的安息地。
　　　　(B) 有時火焰會從岩石裡冒出來。
　　　　(C) 有形似女神的石筍在洞穴裡。
　　　　(D) 島上淡水的來源。

（ C ）3.本文沒有提到下列何種活動？

    (A) 水肺潛水。   (B) 登山健行。

    (C) 賞鯨。   (D) 泡溫泉。

（ D ）4.觀光客在何處可能可以看到野生鹿？

    (A) 洞穴裡。   (B) 溫泉區附近。

    (C) 海岸沿線。   (D) 島中央。

（ A ）5.本文最有可能出現在何處？

    (A) 導覽指南。   (B) 圖書館目錄。

    (C) 醫學期刊。   (D) 新聞稿。

Pop Quiz

1. mysterious   2. spectacular   3. Legend   4. worshipping   5. location

Do You Know!?

海底溫泉好難得

海底溫泉是稀有的地理景觀，已知共有十一個國家有海底溫泉，包括義大利、英國、冰島、烏克蘭、俄羅斯、突尼西亞、挪威、西班牙、日本、法國及臺灣。而類似綠島這種在漲潮時沉沒海中，退潮時才外露的海底溫泉，目前僅在臺灣、日本、義大利三國發現。

我們去露營！

你是否在五天工作日拼命工作，卻把寶貴周末浪費在電視或電腦前？你需要出門走走。我的意思不是在附近公園散步。我說的是露營！

露營近年來已大受歡迎，這是有原因的。這是體驗大自然以及和親朋好友聯絡感情的好方法。但此處有玄機。要想擁有成功的露營行程，你必須做好準備。如果你從來沒露營過，找有經驗的人做伴或參加專業套裝行程。你也需要一張清單，列明該帶的東西。包括優質帳篷、登山鞋、睡袋、防蟲噴霧、雨衣、保暖外套、基礎急救包、烹飪用具和防曬乳液。這還只是新手用的。許多線上露營資源提供完整清單，詳列你會需要的所有東西。出發到野外之前，查詢天候狀況有其必要。例如如果氣象預測說會下大雨，延期旅遊行程是最佳策略。最後，永遠告訴一位朋友或家人，你預計何時結束露營行程返家。

露營可以非常享受，但和任何其他戶外活動一樣，安全第一。露營是消磨週末的好辦法。然而，如同許多人 (包括我在內) 已經發現，露營極易上癮！所以，如果你迷上露營，別說我沒警告過你。

(D) 1. 下列何者是作者建議露營的理由之一？

    (A) 它成為世界上最受歡迎的活動。

    (B) 教你認識野生動物並學習如何養育牠們。

    (C) 這是每個人一生中都必須體驗一次的活動。

    (D) 有助你與家人和朋友更親近。

(C) 2. 根據本文，下列何者是所有露營者都必須做的重要事項？

    (A) 找有經驗的人一起露營。

    (B) 在附近找一個適合露營的公園。

    (C) 露營前做好準備。

    (D) 避免買二手帳篷。

(C) 3. 看起來可能下大雨的話，露營者該怎麼辦？

    (A) 參加套裝行程。

    (B) 持續依計畫進行。

    (C) 延後他們的露營行程。

    (D) 通知他們的家人或朋友。

（ A ） 4.下列關於本文的語氣，何者正確？

　　　⒜ 鼓勵的。　　　　　　　　　⒝ 悲觀的。

　　　⒞ 中立的。　　　　　　　　　⒟ 挑釁的。

（ B ） 5.本文最後兩句，作者意思為何？

　　　⒜ 作者因慘痛的經驗得到教訓。

　　　⒝ 一旦嘗試過露營，就會覺得再多都不滿足。

　　　⒞ 作者建議其他人不要嘗試獨自露營。

　　　⒟ 露營最糟的事是碰上會咬人的蟲子。

Pop Quiz

1. numerous　　2. purchased　　3. recommended　　4. pessimistic　　5. equipment

Do You Know!?

上山露營，勿將廚餘做堆肥

多數人可能會覺得將廚餘埋在土裡讓其自然分解，不僅能堆肥還可以解決垃圾問題。但實際情形卻是，在高海拔低溫的環境下，食物腐化不易，反而會孳生蒼蠅，甚至可能改變當地生態！因此一定要將廚餘帶走喔！

倫敦棒透了！

首站——倫敦塔橋

倫敦塔橋於 1894 年建成，每天約開啟兩次，讓大船通過。我們發現我們剛錯過了一次。

今天的主要活動是搭紅色雙層巴士的觀光行程。我們真的很像觀光客，但不要緊。蠻好玩的，而且這是探索這個城市的好方法。

「帶我們去看英國女王！」結果發現她不在家，所以我們在溫莎古堡拍女王衛隊的照片。

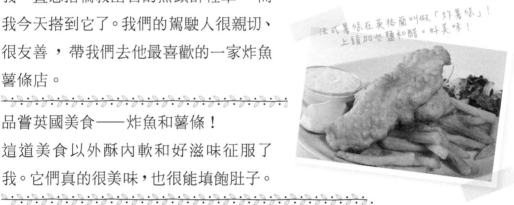
熊皮帽一頂
我要一頂！

我一直想搭倫敦出名的黑頭計程車。而我今天搭到它了。我們的駕駛人很親切、很友善，帶我們去他最喜歡的一家炸魚薯條店。

法式薯條在英格蘭叫做「炸薯條」！上頭加些鹽和醋。好美味！

品嚐英國美食——炸魚和薯條！

這道美食以外酥內軟和好滋味征服了我。它們真的很美味，也很能填飽肚子。

西敏寺
泰晤士河
大笨鐘

猜猜我們在哪裡！倫敦眼的最頂端！大笨鐘、西敏寺、泰晤士河一覽無遺。多棒的方式來結束我們在倫敦特別的一天！

(D) 1.本文主旨為何？

    (A) 這是當地居民寫的日記。

    (B) 這是記者寫的美食評論。

(C) 這是一位觀光客和她的朋友做的旅遊計畫。

(D) 這是觀光客旅行期間寫的旅遊日誌。

(A) 2.作者在溫莎古堡做了什麼事？

  (A) 拍了衛兵的照片。   (B) 參加導覽。

  (C) 進去拜訪女王。   (D) 試戴熊皮帽並拍張照片。

(D) 3.根據本文，下列關於倫敦黑頭計程車的敘述，何者正確？

  (A) 它們可能在不久的未來消失。

  (B) 司機欠缺專業訓練。

  (C) 它們是在倫敦四處逛逛的唯一方法。

  (D) 作者有很好的搭乘經驗。

(C) 4.作者吃炸魚薯條時的感受為何？

  (A) 無聊的。 (B) 噁心的。 (C) 美味的。 (D) 丟臉的。

(B) 5.為何作者喜歡搭倫敦眼？

  (A) 像在搭熱氣球。   (B) 從頂端能看到知名景色。

  (C) 她搭倫敦眼時，大笨鐘敲響了。(D) 作者看到有人在泰晤士河划船。

Pop Quiz

1. sightseeing 2. conquered 3. disgusted 4. residents 5. articles

Do You Know!?

倫敦計程車駕照好難考

想開倫敦黑頭計程車，可沒那麼容易。據統計，平均得花四年才能考到執照，且錄取率不到 2 成。駕駛需通過「知識大全 (The Knowledge)」檢定才能上路。該檢定測驗駕駛對倫敦的熟悉程度。他們需熟記高達 2 萬 5000 條街道和 2 萬個地標位置。即使早已進入衛星導航時代，但倫敦計程車駕駛仍無法被取代。因為他們能客製化乘客的行進路線，不管要到哪裡，司機總是能使命必達。只有你說不出的倫敦地點，沒有他們到不了的地方。

歡迎來到斐濟

珊瑚宮渡假村：您造訪斐濟的最佳選擇

海灘美景加上五星級款待，

這裡是住宿放鬆的完美地點。

有各式優雅套房可選，每晚 400 美元起，包括單人房 / 雙人房和 3 房別墅，所有房間都有海景。每間房都備有平板電視、免費無線上網、空調、冰箱，以及附按摩浴缸的私人衛浴。

別墅包括一間獨立衛浴雙人房和兩間單人房。另有大型起居空間、裝按摩浴缸的衛浴，以及功能齊全的廚房，附爐子、烤箱、微波爐和洗碗機。

我們以能滿足您用餐需求的三家獲獎餐廳為榮。每天，您都能從自助式吃到飽餐廳、精緻酒館和高檔美食餐廳之間，選擇其一。

‧今年 3 月，套裝行程貴賓，每天均可免費享用自助式吃到飽早餐。

我們所有的房間和別墅，都僅距離金色沙灘一分鐘腳程，您可以盡情在那裡游泳和做日光浴，不受打擾。

提供多種水上活動，包括浮潛、潛水、衝浪課程、水上摩托車和沙灘排球。

我們的旅館設備齊全，盡可能讓您的假期便利、輕鬆，有準時的客房服務、乾洗和高效房務整理。

若您想盡情享受斐濟逍遙假期，

入住珊瑚宮渡假村絕對是首選。

欲知更多細節，請至「**www.thecoralpalace.com**」。

(A) 1.本文主旨為何？

(A) 旅館促銷。　(B) 旅館評鑑。　(C) 招募員工。　(D) 旅館出售。

(B) 2.下列何者是內文提到的特殊優惠？

(A) 所有來賓均適用的多種娛樂服務。

(B) 套裝行程貴賓享有免費的吃到飽早餐。

(C) 僅別墅貴客適用的優質客房服務。

(D) 線上預訂別墅的客人可享折扣優惠

(A) 3.下列何者不是所有旅館房間的特色之一？

  (A) 廚房。   (B) 免費 wi-fi。

  (C) 海景。   (D) 平面電視。

(C) 4.根據本文，這家旅館最可能座落何處？

  (A) 山區。   (B) 市中心。

  (C) 海邊。   (D) 湖旁。

(D) 5.何者最可能被這所吸引？

  (A) 喜愛探訪古蹟的旅客。

  (B) 喜歡爬山的旅客。

  (C) 計劃帶嬰兒進行親子遊的旅客。

  (D) 特別受水上活動吸引的旅客。

➡ Pop Quiz

1. punctual 2. distraction 3. hospitality 4. absolute 5. elegant

Do You Know!?

各國電壓與插座孔類型

亞洲	電壓	插頭	歐洲	電壓	插頭
臺灣	110V	A	英國	230V	G
日本	100V	A	法國、德國	230V	C
韓國、中國	220V	C	**美洲**	**電壓**	**插頭**
香港、澳門	220V	G	美國、加拿大	120V	A
新加坡	230V	G	**大洋洲**	**電壓**	**插頭**
馬來西亞	240V	G	澳洲、紐西蘭	230V	I
印尼	230V	C	斐濟	240V	I

A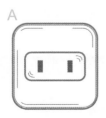 C G I

乳酪蛋糕

每個人都愛乳酪蛋糕。不幸的是，少有美味且價格合理的乳酪蛋糕。而且，商業化生產的乳酪蛋糕通常都加了人工香料。所以，讓我給你幾乎全用奶油乳酪而且有酥脆餅皮的乳酪蛋糕。

時間：	份量：	難度：
7.5 小時	9 吋蛋糕 (12 塊)	簡易

材料

餅皮
* 15 塊消化餅乾 (弄碎)
* 2 茶匙奶油 (融開)

內餡
* 150 克奶油乳酪
* 1 ½ 杯白糖
* ¾ 杯牛奶
* 4 顆蛋
* 1 杯酸奶油
* 1 茶匙天然香草精
* ¼ 杯中筋麵粉 (過篩)

作法：

1. 烤箱預熱至攝氏 170 度。給 9 吋蛋糕烤盤抹上油。
2. 將弄碎的消化餅乾和融開的奶油混合，再將餅乾壓平鋪在抹油的蛋糕烤盤底部。
3. 奶油乳酪加糖攪拌直至滑順。與牛奶混合，每次一顆蛋的加進來，全部混在一起。加進酸奶、香草精和麵粉，然後攪拌所有材料，直到全部混合均勻。
4. 將內餡倒入備好的蛋糕烤盤。
5. 在預熱過的烤箱烤 1 小時。關掉烤箱電源。讓蛋糕在關了門的烤箱裡冷卻 5 到 6 小時。(這樣乳酪蛋糕不會出現裂縫。)
6. 享用之前先把蛋糕送進冰箱冷藏。

試試看！適合每個場合。

(C) 1. 本文寫作形式為何？

　　(A) 菜單。　　　　　　　　　(B) 購物清單。

　　(C) 食譜。　　　　　　　　　(D) 飲食指南。

(D) 2.下列何者不是乳酪蛋糕的材料之一？

    (A) 蛋。   (B) 糖。   (C) 奶油。   (D) 鹽。

(A) 3.使用的烘焙工具為何？

    (A) 烤箱和蛋糕烤盤。   (B) 平底鍋和蛋糕烤盤。

    (C) 湯鍋和量杯。   (D) 平底鍋和量杯。

(B) 4.根據本文，下列敘述何者正確？

    (A) 糖在使用前應該過篩。

    (B) 烤箱應該預熱。

    (C) 對初學者來說做乳酪蛋糕太難。

    (D) 乳酪蛋糕烤 5 至 6 小時以防龜裂。

(D) 5.本文最後兩句，作者的意思為何？

    (A) 叫讀者發揮創意。   (B) 解釋乳酪蛋糕為何美味。

    (C) 強調乳酪蛋糕很貴。   (D) 鼓勵讀者在家隨時可做。

▶ Pop Quiz

1. recipe   2. between   3. Crushing   4. artificial   5. cracked

Do You Know!?

食譜的相關用字

料理方法	sauté (拌炒) pan-fry (煎) stir-fry (快炒) deep-fry (炸) simmer / stew (燉) broil (上火，烤) roast (上下火，烤) grill (烤架，烤)
刀 工	chop (剁、砍) cube (切塊) dice (切丁) mince (絞碎) slice (切片) julienne (切條) shred (切絲)
素	pescetarian (海鮮素) lacto-ovo-vegetarian (蛋奶素) vegan (全素) vegetarian (素食者，不吃肉)

適合住家和辦公室的室內植物

現代人待在室內的時間長，很少接觸大自然。因此，許多人喜歡在家裡或辦公室種點植物。研究顯示，養室內植物可大幅增進空氣品質。根據中國的風水，一些室內植物不僅美觀，同時有其他好處。

發財樹能給主人帶來好財運。一個花盆最多可以種五株發財樹幼苗。成長時可耐心纏繞它們成為一個有著迷人旋轉紋路的樹幹。發財樹很適合種在室內，因其偏好低光照的環境，而且每 7–10 天澆一次水即可。如果室內溼度高，它可能結出可食用的果實和花朵。

另一個和風水大有關係的室內植物是「幸運竹」。據信幸運竹可以讓家裡或辦公室更為寧靜祥和。幸運竹的根數有其深意。例如，如果你想找戀人，挑兩根莖的幸運竹。如果要求財，種 5 根莖！至於希望身體健康的人，種 7 根莖的幸運竹！

(D) 1. 根據本文，為什麼人們喜歡栽種室內植物？

　　(A) 因為那可能是他們宗教信仰的一部分。

　　(B) 那是一種廉價方便的兒童娛樂。

　　(C) 室外沒有足夠空間可讓人們栽種植物。

　　(D) 他們想將大自然和好運帶進家裡或辦公室。

(A) 2. 根據本文，栽種室內植物的優點為何？

　　(A) 空氣較清淨。

　　(B) 和你的衣服很搭。

　　(C) 趕走惡靈。

　　(D) 提供話題。

(C) 3. 下列何者是種發財樹的有趣方法？

　　(A) 如果想戀愛就種兩株。

　　(B) 將發財樹放置暗處，一次最長一週。

　　(C) 趁發財樹成長之際，將數株的樹幹扭編在一起。

　　(D) 把五株發財樹種在不同的花盆裡，觀察會發生什麼事。

(D) 4.根據本文，你該給在家種發財樹的人什麼建議？

  ⒜ 保持葉面溼潤。

  ⒝ 確保空氣乾燥。

  ⒞ 每天早上澆點水。

  ⒟ 別讓它接觸太多陽光。

(B) 5.根據本文，下列何者是你會給求財者的建議？

  ⒜ 吃掉發財樹結的果子。

  ⒝ 種有五根莖的幸運竹。

  ⒞ 在前院種五株小發財樹。

  ⒟ 家裡盡可能的多放植物。

▶ Pop Quiz

1. distinctive 2. entertainment 3. associate 4. romance 5. Research

Do You Know!?

書桌擺得好，書讀得更好!?

把握以下原則，讓你安心讀好書

1.不背對門坐。有人在後方走動容易心神不寧。

2.不背對窗坐。陽光從後方來，易眩目，不易閱讀書籍。

3.盡量不離房門太近。離太近容易被外界聲音影響。

4.座椅一定要有椅背。有靠背支撐背部，才坐得安穩。

5.桌面維持整潔乾淨，不擺放手機或雜物。不然容易受影響而不專心。

荷蘭：自行車騎士的烏托邦

　　要當荷蘭人就是當個自行車騎士。不管去荷蘭的哪裡，都能看到大家騎自行車。這是該國日常生活的一部分。作為提倡綠色運輸的努力環節之一，自行車共享體系在全球各大城市漸受歡迎。然而，荷蘭老早就擁抱自行車，它已經是文化的一部分。

　　荷蘭對自行車的愛戀，可回溯至 1973 年的中東石油危機。都市規劃專家明智決定，要設計出能讓大家騎自行車輕鬆來去的城市和鄉鎮。這造就了自行車道、橋樑和隧道連結起來的大型路網，荷蘭因此成為對自行車很友善的地方。當然，荷蘭地勢出了名的平緩也大有助益。如今，36% 的荷蘭人拿自行車當平日主要的交通工具。國內有各式各樣的自行車道。「自行車大街」給自行車優先權，汽車雖能進入，但時速不得超過 30 公里。「自行車專用道」通常與馬路平行，以路障隔開，例如成排的行道樹。「自行車高速公路」僅自行車可通行，多半是通勤或運動專用。此外，不設交通號誌，且路線不與一般馬路交錯。自行車高速公路又直又平整，特別順暢。

　　拜都市規劃有遠見、交通規則旨在保護自行車騎士和荷蘭人對騎自行車生活有深度自豪感之賜，荷蘭已成為全球的自行車中心。顯然，關於自行車荷蘭有很多東西可以傳授其他國家。

(D) 1.第一段的主旨為何？
　　(A) 荷蘭人很早以前就建立了現代社會。
　　(B) 自行車是解決塞車的最佳方法。
　　(C) 大部分荷蘭人不喜歡汽車。
　　(D) 騎自行車早已是荷蘭文化的一部分。

(A) 2.下列關於荷蘭的敘述，何者正確？
　　(A) 丘陵和高山不多。
　　(B) 至少有 50% 的荷蘭人有兩輛自行車。
　　(C) 荷蘭仰賴中東進口的石油。
　　(D) 荷蘭人被迫騎自行車。

(B) 3.關於「自行車大街」，何者正確？

　　(A) 路上有彎道。

　　(B) 汽車允許駛入。

　　(C) 「自行車大街」與馬路平行。

　　(D) 自行車騎士不得超過時速 30 公里的速限。

(C) 4.第二段的「路線」所指為何？

　　(A) 自行車大街。

　　(B) 自行車專用道。

　　(C) 自行車高速公路。

　　(D) 所有自行車道。

(A) 5.下列何者可由本文推論得知？

　　(A) 其他國家無疑可向荷蘭學習。

　　(B) 荷蘭已經解決中東石油危機。

　　(C) 太多的自行車道、橋樑和隧道，令荷蘭汽車駕駛生氣。

　　(D) 靠自行車通勤的人很快將占荷蘭人口的 36%。

Pop Quiz

1. moreover　　2. priority　　3. popularity　　4. barrier　　5. embrace

Do You Know!?

Go Dutch! 去荷蘭!?

其實「Go Dutch!」指的是「平分」的意思。在 17、18 世紀，英國和荷蘭有十分激烈的海上競爭關係，因此英國常常醜化荷蘭，「Dutch」這個字眼也就多用於貶義的字句。Go Dutch 雖有平分的意思，但原本其實是在諷刺荷蘭人小氣吝嗇。另外有關 Dutch 的字詞還有「Dutch courage」指的是藉喝酒壯膽而來的勇氣，只是一時的虛勇，而非真正的勇氣。

在家帶小孩的代價

1970 和 80 年代，各界積極鼓吹母親追求自己的事業。這讓做母親感覺更自由、獨立和經濟獨立。自 1990 年代以來，追求工作和生活平衡的態度已有轉變，時至今日，部分婦女認為選擇待在家裡照顧小孩，由做父親的出門工作很自在。然而，照顧小孩和做家務雜活，比大部分人想得要難得多。此外，他們不能休假，也完全領不到薪水！

研究顯示，如果母親在家做的每份家務工作都收取報酬的話，從烹飪和接送，到清潔和養育小孩，她的年薪應落在 6 萬美元左右。當你考慮到家庭主婦要做的事，在實質意義上，她是有一份工作的。一個家庭如果雇人來做家庭主婦的所有工作，很可能要花掉全部收入才夠。

當然，不用說，家庭主婦／夫的工作媽媽或爸爸都能擔當。因此，不管父母哪一方決定接受此一挑戰，我們都該花點時間，對他們日復一日擔負這份艱鉅無償的工作，表達感謝之意。

(C) 1. 第一段的主旨為何？

    (A) 已婚男子拒絕擔任全職爸爸。

    (B) 媒體已指示女性成為全職媽媽。

    (C) 操持家務比大部分人以為的要困難。

    (D) 差勁的工作條件令女性選擇待在家裡。

(C) 2. 第二段的主旨為何？

    (A) 雇用女傭的成本上揚。

    (B) 父親應承擔較多責任。

    (C) 家庭主婦／夫做了大量工作。

    (D) 為人父母和養家並不值得。

(D) 3. 根據本文，如果付錢找別人做所有的家務雜活，結果會如何？

    (A) 這個家庭會收到政府福利。

    (B) 這個家庭將必須搬到較大的公寓。

    (C) 大家做決定前必須聯絡律師。

    (D) 這個家庭可能必須花掉所有薪水以付薪給工人。

（　B　）4.最後一段的「挑戰」所指為何？

　　　　(A) 平衡職涯和家庭生活。

　　　　(B) 照顧小孩並操持家務。

　　　　(C) 賺到足夠雇用一個女傭的錢。

　　　　(D) 決定由誰全職留在家。

（　A　）5.作者最後一段的主旨為何？

　　　　(A) 讓我們向家庭主婦／夫表達感激之情。

　　　　(B) 組成一個家庭很可能是相當大的挑戰。

　　　　(C) 時至今日，兩個家長都必須工作養家

　　　　(D) 政府應該支持子女眾多的家庭。

Pop Quiz

1. chores　　2. gratitude　　3. counsels　　4. evolved　　5. career

Do You Know!?

I Want a Wife (By Judy Brady)

作者茱蒂・布雷迪在 "I Want a Wife" 一文中以詼諧諷刺筆法道出她也想要有妻子的理由。文中將妻子描述成可以滿足生活各種需求的工具人。舉凡賺錢養家、洗衣燒飯、宴客款待等；妻子在丈夫完成學業就業前，除了工作也要打理家務。在丈夫終於就業之後，妻子當然就要放棄工作全心家庭。天底下有這麼好的事，誰不想要妻子呢？文章發人省思，讓人重新思考「妻子」的價值與意義。

媽祖將起駕遶境

媽祖遶境即將開始，規模將超越以往。預計將有超過 500 萬名信眾和觀光客參與此為期九天的盛會。

大甲媽祖遶境進香活動，是慶祝在臺灣最受歡迎的神祇，海上女神，媽祖的生日。每年農曆 3 月 23 日，信徒會拜拜、辦桌和辦廟會慶祝。慶典特別關注媽祖鑾轎的行進路線，也就是「她」到各家廟宇巡視臺中境內及周圍轄區。

媽祖神像以及多達 20 萬名信眾，從臺中市大甲鎮瀾宮出發，在返回前的九天期間，繞行中臺灣 300 多公里、停留逾 100 座廟。在每一站，媽祖都受到鞭炮、遊行和表演相迎。據信媽祖神像在各家廟宇遇上其他媽祖神像時，會為那裡的廟宇和民眾帶來好運。

信眾每天走 12 小時，抬著媽祖鑾轎從一座廟到下一座廟。他們收集並綁各廟符令 (一張寫有咒語的紙片) 在令旗上，以表示對媽祖的虔誠心意。

媽祖遶境被聯合國教科文組織視為全球無形資產，而這個文化活動能成為這些資產的其中之一的原因很好理解。想體驗此一盛會的人士，請到 http://www.dajiamazu.org.tw 查詢更多細節。

(A) 1.最適合本文的標題為何？

    (A) 大甲媽祖即將進城。   (B) 大甲媽祖和信徒。

    (C) 恭迎大甲媽祖的方法。   (D) 大甲媽祖遶境與其起源。

(C) 2.第一段的主旨為何？

    (A) 媽祖虔誠信眾的看法。

    (B) 大甲媽祖的意義和起源。

    (C) 大甲媽祖遶境活動的規模。

    (D) 大甲媽祖遶境活動的日期和時間。

(D) 3.根據本文，當媽祖神像在廟裡遇上其它尊媽祖神像，下列何者被認為會發生？

    (A) 其他尊媽祖明年會帶領遶境隊伍。

    (B) 媽祖神像們會被綁在一起 12 個小時。

    (C) 香客和信眾在該期間必須遠離宮廟。

    (D) 會為那裡的廟和人帶來好運。

(C) 4.根據本文，信眾為何收集符令？

    (A) 符令代表好運。

    (B) 代表媽祖沒有到那裡去。

    (C) 表達他們有多崇敬媽祖。

    (D) 燒符令能發財。

(A) 5.最後一段的「無形」所指為何？

    (A) 看不到的。   (B) 個人的。

    (C) 可移動的。   (D) 全國的。

▶ Pop Quiz

1. magnificent   2. corner   3. assets   4. faithful   5. predicted

Do You Know!?

世界三大宗教活動

1. 梵諦岡——子夜彌撒：「彌撒」是天主教的專有名詞，指舉行儀式後信徒在日常生活中實行天主的旨意。梵諦岡的子夜彌撒由教宗主持，每年都有萬名信徒前往參與。

2. 麥加——朝聖之行：伊斯蘭教徒到麥加朝聖的儀式。儀式於伊斯蘭曆 12/8–12/12 舉行。根據經典，每位身體健康、經濟良好的信徒，一生中至少應朝聖一次。

3. 臺灣——大甲媽祖遶境：在當年度的元宵節「筊筶典禮」中擲筊決定遶境的出發日期與時辰 (大約在農曆三月間)。遶境包含十大典禮，筊筶、豎旗、祈安、上轎、起駕、駐駕、祈福、祝壽、回駕及安座，每項典禮都須依既定程序、地點及時間舉行。

愛沙尼亞的年輕程式設計師

我們活在資訊科技時代。從電力供應到智慧手機，複雜的系統都是日常生活中眾多層面的核心。讓這些重要系統運作的語言是電腦代碼。編寫電腦代碼被視為重要技能，歐洲、美國和全球其他許多國家現在都把這種技能教給新一代程式設計師。部分國家，例如中國和愛沙尼亞，甚至從小孩 7 歲就教他們寫程式。

當首次實施全國性的程式設計課程給 7–19 歲的兒童，愛沙尼亞備受矚目。當這些懂得科技語言的學生畢業進入職場時，希望他們的編碼技能能帶來優勢。隨著新科技崛起，愛沙尼亞將因為擁有具編碼技能強大背景的勞動力而受惠。一些歐洲國家，法國、西班牙、斯洛伐克、英國和芬蘭，很快追隨愛沙尼亞的腳步，已將程式設計加入國小課程之中。除擁有程式設計所需技能外，小朋友會學邏輯思考和解決問題的技能，這些也適用資訊科技以外領域。

程式設計是重要性只增不減的國際語言。很難預測未來發展。但有件事很清楚，接下來數十年，不重視從小教程式設計的國家將在全球經濟落於人後。

(C) 1.作者對愛沙尼亞的程式設計教育課程的態度為何？

    (A) 懷有戒心的。   (B) 負面的。

    (C) 支持的。   (D) 漠不關心的。

(B) 2.根據本文，為何有必要教小孩學程式設計？

    (A) 好玩有趣。

    (B) 這是日益重要的技能。

    (C) 能防範小孩打電玩。

    (D) 有助小孩學外國語言。

(B) 3.為何愛沙尼亞備受矚目？

    (A) 愛沙尼亞有全球最優秀的程式設計師。

    (B) 愛沙尼亞開始教導幼童編寫程式。

    (C) 年輕的程式設計師挽救了愛沙尼亞的經濟。

    (D) 愛沙尼亞讓小孩上大學學習編寫程式。

（ A ）4.除編寫程式外，歐洲小學生還學些什麼？

      ⑷ 如何進行邏輯思考。

      ⒝ 如何成為領袖。

      ⒞ 如何製作電腦。

      ⒟ 如何發展人際技巧。

（ C ）5.下列何者可由最後一段推論得知？

      ⑷ 國際教育是蓬勃發展的產業。

      ⒝ 學習編寫程式有可能完全在浪費時間。

      ⒞ 如果各國不教小孩編寫程式，經濟可能受害。

      ⒟ 各國必須增加生產科技產品。

▶Pop Quiz

1. production   2. literate   3. economy   4. aspect   5. vital

Do You Know!?

Code.org 教你學會寫程式

成立於 2013 年的非營利性組織 Code.org，致力推廣電腦科學，鼓勵女性、學生和各膚色群體學習編寫程式。Code.org 提供多國語言、不同難度的免費教學課程讓使用者都能依照自己的需求學習編寫程式。

今夏戲水小心安全

家長們請注意：

如您所知，暑假很快就要到來，我們確信假期間一定會有許多水上活動或出遊。貼心提醒您注意戲水安全，讓孩子今夏安全無虞。

最重要的是孩子必須了解自己的游泳能力，下水後才能做出合宜決定。

海泳會碰上許多游泳池碰不到的挑戰。海泳需要耗費更多力氣，所以確保孩子們知道，游泳池裡做得到的事，海裡做不到。另外，自然的洋流會將人推往特定方向。孩子們必須知道他們相對於海岸的位置。水裡最安全的地方是救生員插旗圍出來的區域。孩子們絕不能游出這個範圍。

儘管游泳池通常是較可控制的環境，但也有其特殊的危險。最常見的問題是在泳池周邊滑倒。這就是為什麼只要當孩子離開池子，就該用走的。另外，他們只能在指定區域跳水，以免撞到池底和與其他游泳者相撞。

更多戲水安全相關資訊，可至 www.swimsafe.gov/childsafety 閱讀。

謝謝，
阿爾巴尼小學

(B) 1.本文主旨為何？

  (A) 提醒學生暑假戲水小心安全。

  (B) 快放暑假了，通知家長戲水安全。

  (C) 準備參加學校為即將來臨的假期規劃的出遊。

  (D) 教老師和學生一些訣竅以免他們在游泳池溺水。

(B) 2.根據本文，下列關於海泳和在泳池游泳的敘述，何者正確？

  (A) 游泳池較危險。   (B) 大海較危險。

  (C) 兩者一樣安全。   (D) 兩者一樣危險。

（ D ）3.下列何者是本文特別提到小朋友海泳時必須留心的事？

　　　　⒜ 附近是否有鯊魚。

　　　　⒝ 是否有保護措施。

　　　　⒞ 他們待在海裡的時間長度。

　　　　⒟ 他們相對於岸邊的位置。

（ C ）4.為何小朋友僅應在泳池的指定區域跳水？

　　　　⒜ 要讓他們守規矩。

　　　　⒝ 防範他們滑倒。

　　　　⒞ 防範他們撞到池底。

　　　　⒟ 不讓他們把水濺得到處都是。

（ A ）5.關於本文，下列何者正確？

　　　　⒜ 這是一封小學發送出來的信。

　　　　⒝ 這是一封教小孩如何游泳的信。

　　　　⒞ 這封信裡能找到個人資料。

　　　　⒟ 這封信應由家長簽名並寄回學校。

▶ Pop Quiz

1. unique　　2. involved　　3. designated　　4. collided　　5. outing

Do You Know!?

比基尼 (Bikini)!?還是臉基尼 (Facekini) 呢!?

比基尼是穿在身上的泳衣，而臉基尼則是戴在臉上的防曬頭套。臉基尼由中國張式范女士發明，為保護在海灘遊玩的人其臉部不被水母螫傷和太陽曬傷。臉基尼在中國青海刮起一陣旋風後，隨即紅遍歐美各地。臉基尼有龍鳳、京劇、青花瓷等多種樣式，提供民眾選購。

常見的 *LINE* 詐騙

以下是戴夫的簡訊摘要。

8月19日(週六)

反詐騙熱線165:

貼心提醒您有關 LINE 上面的常見詐騙。如果 LINE 的朋友開口借錢,永遠保持警覺。如果 LINE 的朋友請你輸入四位數密碼,幾乎一定是詐騙。這表示可能有人竊取了你朋友的 LINE 帳號。你若輸入密碼,其實是允許對方也能掌控你的 LINE 帳號。有任何問題的話,請撥 165 至反詐騙熱線。(下午 12:30)

8月20日(週日)

艾美:嗨,戴夫!我目前有點小麻煩,需要你幫忙。(下午 1:00)

戴夫:出了什麼事?(已讀,下午 1:05)

艾美:其實我現在在醫院。我騎機車出了車禍。不嚴重,但我需要一點錢付醫院帳單。(下午 1:05)

戴夫:健保應該有給付。(已讀,下午 1:05)

艾美:沒錯。不幸的是,我弄丟了健保卡,在補辦前需支付現金。等文書工作完成後,就能把錢拿回來。(下午 1:08)

戴夫:你需要多少錢?(已讀,下午 1:10)

艾美:新台幣 2 萬 8 千 5 百元。你能幫我嗎?拜託!我的銀行帳戶號碼是 904–306–12001。你會收到我銀行的簡訊,要求你確認手機號碼。只要輸入四位數密碼就行。我下週就會還你錢,我保證。(下午 1:10)

8月20日(週日)

戴夫:嗨,琳達!在嗎?(已讀,下午 1:10)

琳達:怎麼回事? (下午 1:11)

戴夫:你和艾美在野餐,不是嗎?(已讀,下午 1:11)

琳達: 她就在我旁邊。出了什麼事嗎?(下午 1:11)

戴夫:哦,沒事!「艾美」剛傳簡訊給我,她出了車禍要借錢。 (已讀,下午 1:12)

琳達: 別擔心!沒事。(下午 1:12)

戴夫:謝謝!玩得開心!(已讀,下午 1:12)

(A) 1.下列何者最能形容戴夫的反應

    ⒜ 警覺的。   ⒝ 虔誠的。   ⒞ 愚笨的。   ⒟ 鼓勵的。

(C) 2.反詐騙簡訊在警告什麼事？

    ⒜ 和 LINE 的朋友分享個人訊息。

    ⒝ 打警方熱線以獲知更多資訊。

    ⒞ 在朋友借錢的請求下輸入四位數密碼。

    ⒟ 傳送個人基本資料給還沒有見過面的 LINE 用戶。

(C) 3.根據本文，為何艾美會向戴夫借錢？

    ⒜ 付停車罰款。   ⒝ 修理她的摩托車。

    ⒞ 付她的醫藥費。   ⒟ 買食物去野餐。

(D) 4.戴夫不同意艾美請求的原因可能為何？

    ⒜ 他手邊沒有足夠的現金。

    ⒝ 他不能再使用他的 LINE 帳號。

    ⒞ 他很生氣，因為他沒有受邀參加野餐。

    ⒟ 他記得唸過有關詐騙的警告。

(B) 5.根據簡訊，關於艾美的 LINE 帳號，下列何者可推論得知？

    ⒜ 戴夫已經刪掉那個帳號。   ⒝ 詐欺犯已經操控那個帳號。

    ⒞ 警方已經控制住那個帳號。   ⒟ 那個帳號在琳達的掌控中。

▶ Pop Quiz

1. insurance   2. financial   3. suspicious   4. moment   5. alert

Do You Know!?

簡訊常見英文縮寫

1. btw：by the way (順帶一提)   5. nvm：never mind (別介意)

2. cu：see you (掰)   6. tbh：to be honest (老實說)

3. gtg：got to go (要走了)   7. ttyl：talk to you later (晚點聊)

4. ic：I see. (我知道了)   8. lol：laugh out loud (大笑)

崔西 2 月行程表

SUN	MON	TUE
2/1	2/2	2/3
2/8	2/9 10:00 為「薩德電池」做新的廣告推廣活動 14:00 為「卡萊拉洗髮精」電視廣告進行腦力激盪	2/10 13:30 廣告會議： 瘋狂建立人脈！
2/15 日出！ 在墨爾本觀光！ 飛回桃園。 飛機 20:15 啟程	2/16 休假	2/17 19:00 和戴夫在「馬洛斯老爹」共進晚餐
2/22 和戴夫在綠島露營	2/23	2/24 11:00 接受訪問熱門廣播節目「媒體開講」。首次上全國電台！別緊張！

(B) 1. 下列何者是崔西在 2 月的第一週安排的事？

　　　 (A) 工作面試。　　(B) 去找獸醫。　　(C) 社交晚宴。　　(D) 和男友約會。

(D) 2. 下列何者是崔西計劃墨爾本花時間做的事？

　　　 (A) 創作新廣告。　　　　　　　　(B) 推銷客戶產品。

　　　 (C) 為公司聘請新員工。　　　　　(D) 在展覽會找到新客戶。

(C) 3. 根據本文，下列敘述何者正確？

　　　 (A) 崔西養了隻名叫摩卡的小狗。　(B) 崔西會在墨爾本待五天。

　　　 (C) 崔西有位同事將在 2 月退休。　(D) 崔西 2 月 7 日要和她的寵物去爬山。

(A) 4. 2 月 24 日會發生什麼事？

　　　 (A) 崔西將上全國性的電台節目。　　(B) 崔西那天早上會成為電台 DJ。

　　　 (C) 崔西將和一家媒體公司進行磋商。(D) 崔西要面試一份新工作。

WED	THU	FRI	SAT
2/4 09:30 見新客戶－ 「OK 可樂」	*2/5* 08:30-12:00 新進員工首次受訓	*2/6* 帶摩卡去看獸醫 喵！	*2/7* 07:00 和瑪莉去三貂嶺古道 健行。
2/11 飛往墨爾本 飛機 23:00 起飛 啊！	*2/12* 19:00 和「奇異」的銷售經 理安珀共進晚餐 有前景！	*2/13* 14:30 見新客戶－ 「袋鼠餅乾」	*2/14* 10:00 參加廣告展 找新客戶！ - - - - - - - 早點睡 (最晚 21:00!!!)
2/18 09:00 月度預算會議	*2/19* 08:30-12:00 為新的藝術總監進行 第一輪面試。	*2/20* 20:00 在「琵琶酒吧」 為銷售總監比爾 舉行退休派對	*2/21* 和戴夫在綠島露營
2/25 21:30 和紐約辦公室進行視 訊會議	*2/26*	*2/27* 19:00 牙醫約診	*2/28* 祝我生日快樂！ 和戴夫看電影並共進 晚餐

(B) 5.根據本文，崔西最可能住在何處？

    (A) 墨爾本。   (B) 台北。   (C) 綠島。   (D) 紐約。

▶ Pop Quiz

1. negotiate   2. intends   3. campaign   4. appointment   5. departs

Do You Know!?

三貂嶺車站——臺灣唯一沒有公路可直接抵達的車站

三貂嶺車站站房建於基隆河峽谷上。第一月台地勢很低，第二月台則緊鄰山壁，下雨時月台上還會出現水簾瀑布的奇景。車站外即為基隆河，無聯外道路，乘客得沿著鐵路走到三貂嶺隧道才會到達附近的住家和商店。

來自紐西蘭的問候

嗨，戴夫

　　我來這裡渡假快一週了，目前為止一切都很棒。紐西蘭是美麗的國家。

　　我前幾天都待在皇后鎮，我永遠不會忘記這個地方。積雪蓋頂的群山環繞著深藍湖泊，景色絕美。

　　昨天，我搭「噴射快艇」在峽谷河起伏。坐起來非常刺激。船速很快，迎面而來的強風和水花讓我幾乎張不開眼。駕駛經常急轉彎，激得冰冷河水四處飛濺，每個人都淋得全身溼。

　　前幾天，我到曾被歐洲殖民的古老毛利人聚落。看他們當時如何生活很有意思。他們是堅強戰士，以獵殺大型不能飛行的鳥「摩亞鳥(恐鳥)」為食，幾乎捕食殆盡。這些鳥現已不幸滅絕。另外，我在紀念品店買了毛利人的精美玉雕。

　　明天，我要搭機到北島的奧克蘭。那裡是紐西蘭的最大城市。聽說天空之塔是不錯的景點。據說，那裡超過 300 公尺高，可以清楚鳥瞰奧克蘭。觀光客也可以去高空彈跳，享受躍下大樓的刺激快感。我真的很想試試。

　　再過幾週我就回家了。到時見。

祝一切安好

羅伯

(D) 1. 為什麼羅伯說皇后鎮是令人難以忘懷的地方？

　　　(A) 他有機會見到皇后。

　　　(B) 他在湛藍色的湖裡游泳。

　　　(C) 他看到城鎮被白雪蓋頂。

　　　(D) 他覺得那裡的景色非凡。

(C) 2. 下列何者最能描述搭「噴射快艇」的感受？

　　　(A) 無聊的。　　　(B) 安寧的。　　　(C) 興奮的。　　　(D) 放鬆的。

(B) 3.下列關於摩亞鳥 (恐鳥) 的敘述，何者正確？

　　　⒜ 毛利人捕牠們不是為了當作食物。

　　　⒝ 摩亞鳥是一種不會飛的鳥。

　　　⒞ 我們仍在紐西蘭能找到摩亞鳥。

　　　⒟ 摩亞鳥是紐西蘭國鳥。

(A) 4.第四段的「精美的」最可能是何意？

　　　⒜ 精緻的。　　　⒝ 美味的。　　　⒞ 陰暗的。　　　⒟ 膚淺的。

(D) 5.根據本文，寄出這張明信片後，羅伯接下來最可能做什麼事？

　　　⒜ 買玉雕。　　　　　　　　⒝ 飛回家。

　　　⒞ 參觀博物館。　　　　　　⒟ 自高樓跳下。

▶ Pop Quiz

1. delicate　　2. Jade　　3. extinct　　4. warrior　　5. fantastic

Do You Know!?

奇異果 (Kiwifruit) 原產地是中國

大多數人以為奇異果原產於紐西蘭，但其實本名「獼猴桃」的奇異果原產於中國。但當時奇異果果實酸澀，一般民眾多不食用，只有山上的野猴會摘取。直到 1904 年紐西蘭傳教士帶回它的種子重新栽培，並於近代建立產銷系統後，它才變為我們現在所熟知飽滿味美的奇異果。

臉書演算後面看不見的手

臉書目前有 18.6 億月活躍用戶。這是個了不起的數字，但更了不起的事實是，大部分用戶每天至少瀏覽一次他們的動態消息。臉書利用各種不同的演算法，決定用戶動態消息頁面會出現什麼樣的貼文。鑒於臉書對我們的許多生活面向有重大影響力，這些演算法已成為引發爭議的源頭。

臉書自己的研究顯示，改變動態消息的演算法能讓大家變得較開心或難過。它也可以影響用戶對各式議題的看法。此外，臉書正面臨壓力，要處理該平台上假新聞日益嚴重的問題。因此，臉書如何管理演算法已經成為媒體關注焦點。當然，身為企業，臉書的主要目的是賺錢。演算法就是要鼓勵用戶儘可能久一點留在網站上，然後靠提供合適的廣告賺錢。臉書目前為止在這方面做得很好。光一年，臉書就能賺 100 億美元。然而，它的演算法因此記錄用戶網路瀏覽了什麼，令人心裡發毛。當然，臉書急欲強調其演算法也可以是行善力量。例如最近實施的自殺防治演算法，可能挽救許多性命。

臉書演算法對全球五分之一的成年人口有重大影響力。雖然這家社群媒體巨擘為我們帶來許多好處，但重要的是人們必須知道在一無所知的情況下，生活其實受到這些聰明程式相當程度的影響。

(C) 1. 下列何者可由第一段推論得知？

(A) 臉書受歡迎程度減低。

(B) 一些演算法可能被視為違法。

(C) 臉書用戶動態消息上的貼文經過選擇。

(D) 許多臉書用戶有帳戶但從未使用。

(A) 2. 第一段的「演算法」是什麼意思？

(A) 一組數學法則。　　　　　　　(B) 一系列指導書籍。

(C) 科技機具。　　　　　　　　　(D) 客戶服務原則。

(B) 3. 根據本文，下列何者可能導致臉書用戶出走？

(A) 出現新的社群網站。

(B) 用戶覺得臉書追蹤他們的網路使用狀況。

(C) 動態消息上太多廣告。

(D) 用戶以為臉書只在乎錢。

（ D ） 4.下列何者是臉書聲稱演算法會有的正面效果？

   (A) 協助用戶交新朋友。

   (B) 檢視線上新聞品質。

   (C) 減少廣告數量。

   (D) 防範民眾自殺。

（ B ） 5.最後一段的片語「社群媒體巨擘」所指為何？

   (A) 出版商。   (B) 臉書。

   (C) 假新聞。   (D) 新聞媒體。

➡ Pop Quiz

1. controversy 2. keen 3. remarkable 4. enormous 5. impact

Do You Know!?

臉書常見英文

Facebook 頁面	常用動作
首頁 home	打卡 check in
動態時報 news feed	分享 share
粉絲專頁 fan page	讚 like
聊天室視窗 chat box	按讚 click the Like button
貼圖 sticker	收回讚 unlike
表情符號 emoticon	取消好友 unfriend

反霸凌海報

停止霸凌——說些什麼吧

看看這兩個小孩。左邊那個是惡霸。

意外嗎?別驚訝。

惡霸會做什麼?

關於惡霸,他們通常看起來不像惡霸!

但所有惡霸都有的一個共通點是,他們選擇一個受害者,以殘酷對待他或她為樂。惡霸可能會打人、上網寫些關於同學的刻薄評語或散播惡毒謠言。最重要的,惡霸強迫別人也欺負他們的受害者。

我們如何阻止霸凌?

這是你能出力的地方。是的,就是你,讀這份海報的人。如果你知道有人被霸凌,出個聲。

把這件事告訴學校裡值得信賴的大人。如果你以為最好保持沉默不作聲,你有可能成為下一個受害者。

讓我們通力合作!

想像你是那個受欺凌的人。你不想要有人幫你結束夢魘嗎?惡霸不會罷手,直到有人站出來說:「夠了,停手。」做對的事,幫忙阻止霸凌。

(B) 1.這份海報的主旨為何?

　　(A) 辨認惡霸很容易。

　　(B) 阻止惡霸行為的方法。

　　(C) 所有惡霸都該受到懲罰。

　　(D) 惡霸知道何時說夠了。

(A) 2.惡霸的共通點為何？

　　　(A) 他們選擇一個受害者。　　　　　(B) 他們有夢魘。

　　　(C) 他們總在微笑。　　　　　　　(D) 他們樂於被欺負。

(D) 3.下列何者是海報提到的霸凌方式？

　　　(A) 在班上逗人笑。

　　　(B) 向老師報告霸凌行為。

　　　(C) 阻止小男孩毆打另一個小女孩。

　　　(D) 在網路上說別人壞話。

(A) 4.誰可能是這張海報的目標讀者？

　　　(A) 學生。　　　　　　　　　　　(B) 老師。

　　　(C) 家長。　　　　　　　　　　　(D) 惡霸。

(B) 5.下列何者可由這張海報推論得知？

　　　(A) 惡霸通常看起來憤怒嚇人。

　　　(B) 如果大家保持沉默，惡霸不會停手。

　　　(C) 小孩子之間的霸凌只是無害的遊戲。

　　　(D) 大部分人都有被欺負的經驗。

➤ Pop Quiz

1. identify　2. nightmare　3. common　4. comments　5. nasty

Do You Know!?

霸凌相關英文

網路霸凌 Cyberbully
言語攻擊 Verbal attack
言語暴力 Verbal abuse
網友 Netizen
酸民 Hater

尊重著作權

對著作權法備感困惑？

我們來一探究竟。

　　版權符號通常代表受著作權法保護的作品，你不能未經允許就複製。如果它受到著作權法保護，擅加複製並供商業用途，其實就是違法行為。然而，基於教育目的，複印合理頁數是被允許的。例如，老師可以從詩集裡複印一首詩當講義。學生可以為了學校作業，複印一則新聞報導。這稱之為合理使用。如果你依照這個方式進行複製，永遠都要記得標明出處。

　　牢記銷售或分享有版權作品是非法行為，包括數位版本在內。你不該違反著作權法，否則可能陷入大麻煩。

　　如果你還不清楚，聯絡版權擁有者，請求授權。不管是創意還是有版權的作品都不是免費的。弄清楚並遵循法規是你的責任。

（ B ）1.本文主旨為何？

　　(A) 解釋版權符號的起源。

　　(B) 釐清與著作權相關的一些常見問題。

　　(C) 敦促大家不要使用有版權資料。

　　(D) 教年輕人如何迴避著作權法。

（ A ）2.第一段「合理使用」的意思為何？

　　(A) 把一部分資料拿來做教學使用是合法的。

　　(B) 未付費就使用那些資料並不公平。

　　(C) 所有創意寫作應可免費使用的概念。

　　(D) 保護藝術家和作家的作品免於被擅用的法律。

（ C ）3.根據本文，下列何者正確？

　　(A) 困惑時應聯絡律師。

　　(B) 沒有版權符號，人們不能複製資料。

　　(C) 使用他人作品，最安全的方法是聯絡版權擁有者。

　　(D) 版權權號警告大家不要複製任何資料。

（ D ）4.下列何者不受著作權法保護？

　　　　(A) 新聞報導。

　　　　(B) 印在詩集裡的詩。

　　　　(C) 出版了的小說其中一章。

　　　　(D) 你母親寫的購物清單。

（ A ）5.本文最後一句話，作者的意思為何？

　　　　(A) 了解並尊重版權，人人有責。

　　　　(B) 複製導致違反著作權法是很糟的事。

　　　　(C) 你應一直假設著作權律師在盯著你。

　　　　(D) 當有人違反著作權法，通知警方是我們的責任。

Pop Quiz

1. material　　2. clarify　　3. concept　　4. published　　5. permissible

Do You Know!?

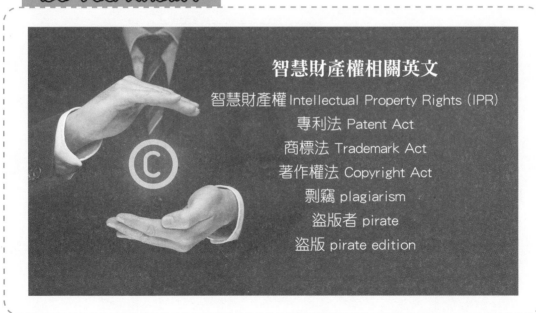

智慧財產權相關英文

智慧財產權 Intellectual Property Rights（IPR）

專利法 Patent Act

商標法 Trademark Act

著作權法 Copyright Act

剽竊 plagiarism

盜版者 pirate

盜版 pirate edition

來救狗狗！

地點：國王公園

日期：4/7 (六)、4/8 (日) 時間：10:00－16:00

　　來吧！和至少 50 隻迫切需要家的狗狗和幼犬一起玩耍。有大小和性格不一的狗狗，適合各種家庭，每隻狗都已結紮並除蟲。我們也提供工作營，給予訓練和照顧你新伙伴的內行建議。

　　每天都有抽獎，只要捐款給「為流浪動物祈福」基金會的人就有機會贏得多種狗狗配件，包括狗床和優質狗糧。

> －高達 50 隻狗等候收養
>
> 　　註冊費：1.微晶片植入——台幣 250 元
>
> 　　　　　　2.狂犬病疫苗——台幣 300 元
>
> －教導如何照顧新寵物的工作坊
>
> －每日抽獎
>
> －手工製狗狗配件和玩具大特賣
>
> －美味熱狗

已有這麼多狗待援，何必買幼犬？

最完美的寵物正等你帶牠回家。

為流浪動物祈福基金會主辦

電子郵件信箱：prayforstrays@gmail.com

(B) 1. 這個活動的主旨為何？

　　(A) 抽獎。　　　　　　　　　　(B) 領養狗狗。

　　(C) 為流浪動物祈福。　　　　　(D) 銷售寵物配件。

(A) 2. 工作坊的目的為何？

　　(A) 如何養寵物。

　　(B) 如何幫助流浪狗。

　　(C) 如何製作狗項圈和玩具。

　　(D) 如何讓狗接種疫苗。

（ C ）3.第一段裡的「伙伴」所指為何？

　　　　(A) 賣熱狗的人。

　　　　(B) 工作坊的工作人員。

　　　　(C) 被領養的狗。

　　　　(D) 這場活動的捐款人。

（ D ）4.下列訊息，何者沒有列在宣傳單上？

　　　　(A) 聯絡資訊。

　　　　(B) 時間和地點。

　　　　(C) 主動單位和活動。

　　　　(D) 入場費。

（ D ）5.如果想贏得狗狗配件，應該先做何事？

　　　　(A) 領養一隻狗。　　　　　　(B) 買熱狗。

　　　　(C) 參加工作坊。　　　　　　(D) 捐款給基金會。

Pop Quiz

1. lottery　　2. foundation　　3. donating　　4. desperate　　5. strays

Do You Know!?

TNVR 是什麼？

你聽過「以領養代替購買、以結紮代替撲殺」這句口號，那你知道 TNVR 是什麼嗎？相較於以往安樂死流浪動物，TNVR 指的是 Trap→Neuter→Vaccinate→Return（誘捕、結紮、注射疫苗、回置），希望藉由此較人道方式管理逐步減少流浪動物數量和其衍生問題。

今晚收看，認識人權！

和平╳人權
剛剛 · 🌏

人權很脆弱。所以即使你是住在重視人權的自由國度，人權永遠是重要的討論議題。

這是為什麼我們很高興宣布，本週將主辦五場人權系列演講。每場演講長兩小時，晚上 7:30 開始，會在臉書直播。

我們的第一位講者是洛杉磯加州大學知名法學教授以及人權鬥士，傑佛瑞·泰德。他很出名，因為在許多涉及 (美國憲法) 第一修正案的重要訴訟案裡擔任要角。從他的經驗，泰德教授今晚將談社會有言論自由的重要性。傑佛瑞是真正全心投入的活躍份子，持續為人權奮鬥，特別是言論自由。

今晚 7:30 務必收看我們的臉書直播。不要忘記按讚並分享這則貼文，這樣就有機會免費獲得一個人權杯墊。

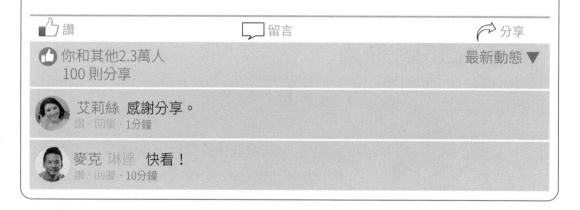

👍讚　　　　💬留言　　　　↪分享

👍 你和其他2.3萬人　　　　　　　　　　最新動態 ▼
100 則分享

艾莉絲　感謝分享。
讚 · 回覆 · 1分鐘

麥克 琳達　快看！
讚 · 回覆 · 10分鐘

(A) 1.總共有幾場演講，本文提到的是哪一場？

　　　(A) 5 場，第一場。　　　　　　(B) 5 場，第二場。

　　　(C) 4 場，第一場。　　　　　　(D) 4 場，最後一場。

(D) 2.這場演講何時結束？

　　　(A) 7:30。　　　(B) 19:30。　　　(C) 9: 30。　　　(D) 21:30。

(D) 3. 第三段的「(美國憲法) 第一修正案」所指為何？

    (A) 隱私權。   (B) 學校政策。

    (C) 法律學位。   (D) 和言論自由有關的法律。

(A) 4. 如何才能贏得免費杯墊？

    (A) 按讚並分享貼文。

    (B) 收看講座的臉書直播。

    (C) 在直播時留言。

    (D) 收看所有演講並回答問題。

(B) 5. 根據貼文，下列何者正確？

    (A) 在已開發國家，人們享有較多自由，不需要真的在乎人權。

    (B) 不管住在哪個國家或地區，人們應該在乎人權議題。

    (C) 傑佛瑞非常高興看到社會正義議題受歡迎，並且獲得正面迴響。

    (D) 傑佛瑞在人權領域是優秀專家；沒有他，(美國憲法) 第一修正案永遠不會通過。

➤ Pop Quiz

1. privacy   2. fragile   3. crucial   4. tune   5. campaigning

Do You Know!?

現代民權運動之母──羅莎・帕克斯

1900 年代，美國蒙哥馬利市的法案規定在公車上仍區分白人、黑人座位區。根據法案，當座位滿座時黑人乘客需讓座給白人乘客。1955 年 12 月 1 日，公車司機要求帕克斯將其座位讓給白人乘客，帕克斯因拒絕司機的指令而遭警方逮捕。此事件引發人們抵制公車運動並帶動一連串的抗爭活動。爾後羅莎・帕克斯便成為民權運動的精神領袖，被稱為「現代民權運動之母」。

單一故事和刻板印象

　　奈及利亞作家切馬曼達・戈齊・阿迪切到美國唸大學時，她的室友很意外她知道如何使用爐子。切馬曼達很快理解，她的室友對非洲的認識僅是單一故事。在她廣為人知的 TED 演講上，切馬曼達解釋單一故事的危險性：「單一故事創造刻板印象，刻板印象的問題不在於那並非實情，而是不完整。它們讓一個故事變成了唯一的故事。」

　　不管喜不喜歡，我們對周遭世界都存有單一故事。身為一個住台灣的外國白人，我有親身體驗。出自某些我從來不了解的怪異原因，台灣人經常假設我是美國人。這是住台灣的白人會有的單一故事。當我解釋我來自英國，另一個摻有霧、雨水、倫敦和紳士的故事取而代之，一堆和我的祖國相關的簡單刻板印象。你可能好奇，我 1993 年來台灣之前，對台灣的單一故事是什麼。事實上，我對這個國家簡直一無所知，除了知道它生產便宜貨以外。不幸的是，即使這個關於台灣的單一故事不再正確，許多不熟悉台灣過去數十年成就的人，心裡還是這樣想。

　　我們該怎麼避免單一故事的危險呢？關鍵是檢視自己對世界和其他人的看法。跳脫刻板印象，它們才會開始消失。

（　D　）1. 為什麼切馬曼達的室友很意外她會用爐子？

　　　(A) 語言障礙對她來說很困難。

　　　(B) 她只是在講笑話來打破冷場。

　　　(C) 她希望有人能教她做飯。

　　　(D) 她很可能以為非洲人沒有爐子。

（　B　）2. 第二段的主旨為何？

　　　(A) 作者對台灣最初的認知。

　　　(B) 作者有關文化刻板印象的個人經驗。

　　　(C) 作者生氣別人對英國的誤解。

　　　(D) 作者在台灣讀到的傳統故事。

（ A ）3.根據本文，台灣的單一故事為何？

    (A) 生產便宜貨的國家。

    (B) 有豐富文化遺產的小島。

    (C) 亞洲最先進的工業國家之一。

    (D) 永遠籠罩了一層霧的地方。

（ C ）4.下列關於切馬曼達的敘述，何者不正確？

    (A) 她不是一個住在台灣的外國白人。

    (B) 她在美國接受高等教育。

    (C) 她在美國學會給爐子點火。

    (D) 她演講談單一故事的危險。

（ B ）5.本文作者現居何處？

    (A) 奈及利亞。   (B) 台灣。

    (C) 美國。   (D) 英國。

Pop Quiz

1. manufacturing   2. conception   3. initial   4. persisted   5. Virtually

Do You Know!?

We Should All Be Feminist (By Chimamanda Ngozi Adichie)

奈及利亞作家切馬曼達‧戈齊‧阿迪切在 TED 的另一則演講 "We Should All Be Feminist" 也同樣引起了廣大迴響並出版同名書籍。演講闡述她在成長過程中因女性身分而遭受的不平等待遇。切馬曼達認為女權主義者不分男女，只要認為現今社會仍存在性別問題且想要修正它們的人就可以是女權主義者。我們應當拒絕、抗議那些不合理的事，一起成為一位「更好」的人。

Unit 21

台灣原住民語言正在消失

約 400 年前，從中國來的人渡海到台灣，展開新生活。那時，台灣原住民人口相當少。他們總共說 42 種語言，但隨歲月流失，能說這些語言的人數減少。時至今日，原本的 42 種中有 9 種原住民語言瀕臨永久消失。

語言和文化息息相關。當少數民族的文化受到另一個較佔優勢文化的影響，其語言也將受到威脅。這是發生在全球各地的趨勢。在某些地區，僅有少數人能說特定語言。等他們過世，那個語言如果沒有傳授給年輕世代也將死去。例如，台灣的撒奇萊雅族人口不足 700。它的語言因為少有人講而受到威脅。台灣原住民族委員會一直努力防範這些語言凋零。損失的將不只是語言還有文化，因為這些語言經常傳遞當地動植物的有用知識。

台灣正探尋不同的方法以保存這些瀕危語言。其中一個挑戰是想出一套書寫系統，讓學習者不必只靠口語。讓我們期待研究人員能達成這個重要工作。

（ A ）1. 下列何者最能描述作者對保存原住民語言的態度？

　　⒜ 關心的。

　　⒝ 懷有戒心的。

　　⒞ 負面的。

　　⒟ 樂觀的。

（ A ）2. 根據本文，下列關於撒奇萊雅族的事，何者正確？

　　⒜ 它的語言可能很快滅絕。

　　⒝ 那裡的動植物滅絕了。

　　⒞ 那裡的人不保護自己的語言。

　　⒟ 9 種他們的語言瀕臨消失。

（ C ）3. 根據本文，除文化因素以外，為什麼原住民語言很重要？

　　⒜ 他們可以吸引觀光客來台。

　　⒝ 他們可以防範死亡和疾病。

　　⒞ 他們有當地野生生物的資訊。

　　⒟ 他們為原住民族委員會募款。

（　D　）4.最後一段的「重要工作」所指為何？

　　　　　(A) 找出自艱困處境獲利的方法。

　　　　　(B) 開發一種世界通用語言以分享知識。

　　　　　(C) 保護從原住民那裡取得的土地。

　　　　　(D) 創造一種系統，以便書寫並保存原住民語言。

（　D　）5.本文最可能取自下列何處？

　　　　　(A) 商業期刊。

　　　　　(B) 科學雜誌。

　　　　　(C) 語言學習指南。

　　　　　(D) 原住民文化專書。

Pop Quiz

1. endangered　　2. universal　　3. conveyed　　4. explored　　5. decreasing

Do You Know!?

原住民族日──8月1日

在原住民族及各界不斷的努力下，政府於 1994 年 8 月 1 日增修憲法條文將「山胞」正名為「原住民」。為了讓大家對原住民有正確認知，行政院在 2005 年將每年 8 月 1 日定為「原住民族日」，希望藉此讓臺灣真正成為多元文化的社會。

博愛座：贊成還是反對

以下是訪談摘錄。

> 主持人：公共運輸工具上的博愛座通常保留給有特殊需求的人，例如老弱婦孺。然而，幾次事件凸顯博愛座的一些問題。一個案例是一位失明男子坐博愛座遭到騷擾，因為他不是明顯看得出來的身障人士。此外，一位年輕女士坐博愛座也備受指責。但其實她懷孕三個月。這一類的事件導致大家抗議反對博愛座。另有近 7000 人簽名請願，呼籲公共運輸系統取消博愛座。李教授，你對此事的看法為何？
>
> 李教授：這個嘛，對我來說，似乎反應過度。畢竟，博愛座的目的是提供座位給有需要的人。如果取消就是把嬰兒和洗澡水一起倒掉。
>
> 主持人：有趣的論點，但那些不是老弱婦孺的人怎麼辦呢？他們也可能有特殊需求。你不認為博愛座這項作法歧視那些人嗎？
>
> 李教授：公共運輸不可能人人都覺得滿意。但我認為，博愛座的優點多於潛在缺點。當然，這個系統需要改善，但如我所說，全盤摧毀有點太過頭。我也想說，這更是溝通的問題。如果大家能多溝通，讓別人知曉他們的需求，一些衝突很可能避得掉。
>
> 主持人：對一些人來說，當眾表達需求有難度，也許這就是事件發生的原因。好的，我們今天時間已到。讓我們擱置歧見。李教授，感謝您和我們分享看法。

(B) 1.教授對於取消博愛座的立場為何？

 (A) 贊成的。

 (B) 反對的。

 (C) 中立的。

 (D) 漠不關心的。

(A) 2.下列何者令民眾籲請取消博愛座？

 (A) 一位男性盲人遭他人錯誤指控。

 (B) 一位懷孕婦女讓座給老人。

 (C) 民眾抗議反對博愛座。

 (D) 政府對博愛座有新政策。

(D) 3.教授在第一個回應中所說的「把嬰兒和洗澡水一起倒掉」，所指為何？

    (A) 保留一個壞主意，因為有個小優點。

    (B) 保留一個好主意，因為有很多優點。

    (C) 摒棄一個壞主意，因為有缺點。

    (D) 摒棄一個好主意，因為有個小缺點。

(C) 4.主持人的訪談結論為何？

    (A) 交通局應做決定。

    (B) 主持人將邀請一位交通局官員擔任來賓。

    (C) 主持人和李教授可能對博愛座有歧見，但他們互相尊重。

    (D) 少數服從多數，由民眾決定是否保留或取消博愛座。

(D) 5.可由此次訪談推論得知何事？

    (A) 主持人和教授同意取消博愛座。

    (B) 訪談是為了討論公共安全。

    (C) 大眾運輸是為老年人和身障者所設計。

    (D) 李教授認為真正的問題在於溝通，不在博愛座。

➡ Pop Quiz

1. potential　　2. discriminated　　3. protest　　4. accused　　5. communication

Do You Know!?

讓座禮儀大不同

英國：對長者、孕婦、殘障人士一視同仁。但會讓座給有需求者。

德國：除非對方開口詢問是否願意讓座，不然讓座反而是種不禮貌。

美國：不特別讓座給長者，主動讓座會給對方被歧視的感覺。

日本：大多情況下不主動讓座給長者，貿然讓座會造成對方尷尬也可能讓
　　　對方覺得自己是不是看起來很老。

韓國：十分強調長幼有序，若不主動讓座給長者會挨罵。

搬遷告示

媽媽咪呀即將搬遷！

我們在薛爾曼街 244 號找到新家！

就在兩條街外。請看下面的地圖，有更詳細的方向！

新店！　金百利路　　高地路

薛爾曼街

新地點有：

♨ 二樓可辦私人派對或其他活動。

♨ 自己的停車場，共 26 個車位。就在隔壁！

♨ 擴建過的超棒新廚房，將推出更多菜式。

　我們現在提供您喜歡的老口味和更多特餐！

♨ 全新窯烤爐！每天供應新鮮麵包和披薩！

📢 最後一天的派對是在 4 月 8 日 (週六)。

　所有用餐來賓享有免費飲料一杯，口味自選！(葡萄酒或碳酸飲料)

📢 新店將於 4 月 28 日 (週五) 盛大重新開幕。

　將有位非常特別的神祕嘉賓到場。而且，當然會有特殊優惠。敬請造訪我們的粉絲頁，查詢重新開幕詳情 www.mammamiarestaurant.com

我們很感謝您，我們的忠實顧客。

因為有您，媽媽咪呀已成為我們超棒社區的一分子。

媽媽咪呀

(C) 1.這張告示的主旨為何？

      (A) 推出特價優惠來宣傳餐廳。   (B) 歡迎用餐者嘗試新特色餐。

      (C) 通知顧客媽媽咪呀的變化。   (D) 宣布在薛爾曼街開新分店。

(A) 2.根據告示，媽媽咪呀的停車場會在哪裡？

      (A) 就在餐廳隔壁。   (B) 距離一條街的地方。

      (C) 在餐廳後面。   (D) 在餐廳對面。

(B) 3.告示提到關於新廚房的事為何？

      (A) 不理想。   (B) 大得多。

      (C) 花很多錢蓋。   (D) 沒有烤爐。

(A) 4.用餐來賓到新地點可期待下列何者？

      (A) 新鮮烘焙的麵包。   (B) 較年輕的主廚。

      (C) 菜單漲價。   (D) 菜單菜色減少。

(B) 5.關於媽媽咪呀的舊地點，下列何者可由告示推論得知？

      (A) 提供更多座位給用餐來賓。   (B) 是一層樓的餐廳。

      (C) 會變成時裝店。   (D) 比新地點好。

Pop Quiz

1. enlarge   2. brand   3. community   4. expands   5. loyal

Do You Know!?

歐盟認證的 STG 披薩，給你義大利原汁原味

STG (義文：Specialità tradizionale garantita) 的意思是「傳統特色證明」，在 STG 的標準下做出來的披薩，就是正宗的拿坡里披薩。STG 披薩形狀需為直徑 30–35 公分之間的圓形且外圍需膨脹鬆軟。麵團成分比例為水 (1L)、海鹽 (50～55g)、酵母 (3g)、00 號或 0 號麵粉 (1.7～1.8kg)。混合發酵後的麵團必須經雙手 (不用任何工具) 延展成麵皮。餡料材料需為聖馬爾扎諾番茄糊、莫扎瑞拉起司、特級初榨橄欖油。最後以燒木材的窯爐烘烤 (溫度 400～480°C、時間 60～90 秒)。

選我進費爾科技

山米‧布洛克
加利福尼亞州威尼斯區墨菲路 1705 號，郵遞區號 90291
電話：1-802-5551234
電子郵件：sammybrock@sanminmail.com

---

2 月 23 日，2018 年

克蘿伊‧羅賓森

聘僱經理

加利福尼亞州洛杉磯市艾瑟南克路 58 號，郵遞區號 90024

羅賓森小姐您好，

身為一個驗驗豐富的軟體工程師，我了解創新對軟體開發的重要性，特別是貴公司在尖端科技市場中的自我定位。費爾科技奮力追求進步，我可以協助費爾科技更往前邁進。

為什麼選費爾科技

現今談到新軟體開發商，費爾科技絕對領先群倫。沒有什麼比得過一家強勁的新創公司的活力環境，能夠鼓勵創造力，給予員工追求自我創意的自由。這是為什麼我熱切盼望成為這家日益茁壯公司的一份子。

我的經驗

自史丹佛大學電腦系畢業後，我已在多家出名軟體公司任職。

- 在 Ensemble，我領頭開發雲端資料庫。
- 在 Obisoft，我為大型多人線上角色扮演遊戲《黑暗地平線》設計網路代碼。

我對資料庫和網路系統的技巧都很熟練，而且我擅長 12 種程式語言。

為什麼選我

程式設計是我的生命。最愉悅的事莫過於團隊合作追求共同目標，緩慢但踏實的從無變成有價值的事物。基於上述，我不僅了解獲致成果要付出什麼，更重要的，可能是了解到什麼狀況不會有成果。我對能夠激勵自己和他人加倍努力，感到自豪。我堅定相信在每一方面都要追求卓越。

誠摯的，

山米‧布洛克

(D) 1.本文語氣為何？

    (A) 悲觀的。   (B) 謹慎的。   (C) 謙卑的。   (D) 熱情的。

(B) 2.作者如何形容費爾科技？

    (A) 一間 Obisoft 的分公司。   (B) 是業界的明日之星。

    (C) 是業界老公司。   (D) 善於生產電腦。

(A) 3.作者擅長下列何者？

    (A) 電腦程式設計。   (B) 玩遊戲。

    (C) 學習外國語言。   (D) 公司發展。

(C) 4.根據本文，下列關於作者，何者正確？

    (A) 他不擅長編寫程式。

    (B) 他能說 12 種外語。

    (C) 他對這份工作的態度很積極。

    (D) 他曾效力 Ensemble 並負責氣象研究。

(B) 5.本文最可能是下列何者？

    (A) 故事。   (B) 求職信。   (C) 廣告。   (D) 新聞報導。

Pop Quiz

1. passionate   2. innovation   3. striving   4. horizon   5. pursuit

Do You Know!?

主管職稱對照

執行長 CEO (Chief Executive Officer)

營運長 COO (Chief Operating Officer)

財務長 CFO (Chief Financial Officer)

行銷長 CMO (Chief Marketing Officer)

搞定求職面試的七個方法

如果你在求職面試時表現不佳，天分、經驗和資格條件恐怕也沒什麼用處。以下是準備求職面試的七個重要步驟。它們會給你競爭優勢。

1. 研究公司——了解這個組織做些什麼、如何運作，對合宜回答面試問題至關重要。

2. 符合你的條件——知道這個組織在找什麼特定技能。讓面試官看到你符合這份工作的所有要求及你了解在未來職位上，公司對你有何要求。

3. 練習回答常見問題——準備常見面試問題的答案。「你的最大長處／短處？」、「跟我談談你自己。」、「為什麼我該聘用你？」是一些熱門的問題。給面試官好的答案是留下好印象的最佳方法。

4. 知道該穿什麼——穿著得體！依照去面試的公司性質來選擇要穿的衣服。但務必記得留心打扮，並熨燙你選的服裝。

5. 有所準備——永遠多帶一份印在高品質紙張上的履歷表與推薦信和作品集。帶著筆記本和筆也會很方便。

6. 小心肢體語言——小心非語言的提示。維持良好體態，看起來有自信。要專心，但不要瞪人。

7. 提問——最後，準備要問的問題。別問那些只要上他們官方網站或其它可得資源就能輕鬆解答的問題。

　　面試前做這七件事，是讓你想要的工作手到擒來的有效方法。

(D) 1. 本文主旨為何？
  (A) 如何給人面試。   (B) 面試的重要性。
  (C) 面試的優缺點。   (D) 準備面試的訣竅。

(C) 2. 本文如何提出構想？
  (A) 利用數字和符號。 (B) 提供不同意見。
  (C) 一個個列舉。   (D) 利用真實情境下的案例。

(B) 3.關於作者說穿什麼，下列何者正確？

    (A) 穿著休閒。   (B) 看起來整齊乾淨。

    (C) 穿著亮色套裝。   (D) 換上最貴的衣服。

(B) 4.下列關於該帶什麼，何者沒被提及？

    (A) 作品集。   (B) 身分證件影本。

    (C) 筆和紙。   (D) 備份履歷表。

(A) 5.根據本文，下列關於求職者面試前必須完成的工作何者正確？

    (A) 準備好常見問題的答案。

    (B) 準備問題，其答案要輕鬆就能找到。

    (C) 在朋友或家人面前練習如何講話。

    (D) 練習肢體語言。學習瞪著面試官。

▶ Pop Quiz

1. competition   2. postures   3. impression   4. prospective   5. spare

Do You Know!?

面試三技巧，教你留下好印象

Tip 1 開場結束謝謝您：開始面試和結束面試離開前請不忘和面試官表達謝意。感謝對方提供此次面試機會和寶貴時間。

Tip 2 聚焦主題不失焦：自我介紹和回答問題時，除了展現自我特質外，也要會察言觀色，針對面試官感興趣部份加以闡述。答題也要好酒沉甕底，切忌開頭就把所有事蹟全部說完，避免有在炫耀的感覺，也可讓答案不虎頭蛇尾。

Tip 3 事實勝於雄辯：千萬不要空口說白話，過度吹噓自己的能力。與其說自己能力有多好，不如提出證照、績效數字等實證，證明自己所言不假。談話時也要自信不畏縮害羞或驕傲自滿。

恆星客戶服務

以下是兩封信件。

收件人：	恆星客服
寄件人：	麥克・劉
主旨：	筆記型電腦維修

親愛的恆星客服，

去年 1 月，我購買了一台恆星 B120x 筆電。原本運作無礙。然而，一週前開始，只要我使用超過半小時，這台筆電就會發出很多噪音，最終當機。我注意到它變得很燙。我的一位朋友說，這台筆電過熱，需要維修。

我覺得十分沮喪，才用一年，這麼貴的產品竟然會有這些問題。我期待所有維修和可能必要的新零件都不收費。我的保固卡號碼是 394839375。我希望這台筆電能儘快維修好，因為我工作還要使用。

誠摯的，
麥克・劉

收件人：	麥克・劉
寄件人：	恆星客服
主旨：	回覆：筆記型電腦維修

親愛的劉先生，

很抱歉聽到，您 1 月 10 日購買的恆星 B120x 筆電無法正常運作。我們的一位技術人員已經看過您的來信，您的筆電出的問題很常見，能修得好。

不幸的是，我們無法免費維修，因為 12 個月的保固期在一個月前到期了。如果您想要我們修理這台筆電，必須拿到恆星的直營門市檢修。

請注意，不管您選擇修或不修，檢測費是 25 美元。我們也必須將您的筆電留置過夜，我們的工作人員才能執行必要的診斷測試。

謝謝您。

誠摯的，
恆星客服

(D) 1.麥克的筆電問題為何？

　　(A) 電池沒電。　　　　　　　　(B) 未正常啟動。

　　(C) 畫面很快停住不動。　　　　(D) 發出噪音並當機。

(B) 2.關於保固期，何者正確？

　　(A) 仍有效。　　　　　　　　　(B) 已過期。

　　(C) 保固卡號碼是 B120x。　　　(D) 恆星公司拒絕給予保固。

(D) 3.下列何者可由這兩封信推論得知？

　　(A) 恆星客服素質不好。　　　　(B) 恆星能滿足麥克的要求。

　　(C) 恆星會派人去拿壞掉的筆電。 (D) 麥克閱讀回信後可能感到失望。

(B) 4.如果檢測後，麥克發現負擔不起修理費，決定不修了，他該付多少錢？

　　(A) 12 美元。　　(B) 25 美元。　　(C) 120 美元。　　(D) 不用收費。

(D) 5.這兩封信最可能的下筆的月份為何？

　　(A) 11 月。　　　(B) 12 月。　　　(C) 1 月。　　　(D) 2 月。

Pop Quiz

1. warranty　　2. regardless　　3. inspection　　4. demands　　5. overnight

Do You Know!?

各種署名敬辭 sign-offs

隨興↓正式	1. Love,：親近，用於家人、情侶、朋友間通信。
	2. Cheer, / Take Care,：隨興，用於朋友間通信。
	3. Yours, / Yours truly, / Truly,：用於日常或工作場合往來。(認識收件者)
	4. Best, / Best wishes,：用於日常或工作場合往來。(認不認識收件者皆可)
	5. Sincerely, / Sincerely yours,：日常、商業到正式書信皆可使用。
	6. (Best) Regards,：用於商業或正式書信，通常用於你沒有見過收件者時。
	7. Cordially,：用於主題嚴肅的正式商業信函。

春酒聚餐快到了

以下是兩封信件。

收件人：	全體員工
寄件人：	人力資源部
主旨：	春酒晚宴調查

全體員工大家好，

希望你們農曆新年都很愉快。為了慶祝新年度開始，我們將在未來幾週辦春酒晚宴。日期和場地未定，將投票表決。每位想參加的員工需回函說明他們偏好的日期和餐廳。餐廳和日期明列如下，以供選擇。

日期：2/28 (週一)、3/1 (週二)、3/2 (週三)、3/3 (週四)、3/4 (週五)

餐廳：

中式	日式	美式	義式
美食宮殿	壽司吧	美味	天堂披薩

儘管在訂位之前，晚宴時間無法定案，但應該落在晚上 6:00–8:00 之間。

等日期、時間和場地都確認後，想出席的人應該告知人力資源部，我們也好通知餐廳預期人數。

對於不能參加的人，我們預先致歉。謝謝。

收件人：	全體員工
寄件人：	人力資源部
主旨：	春酒晚宴調查結果

全體員工請注意，

我們的春酒晚宴投票結果出爐，日期和餐廳都已經決定。

我們很榮幸宣布，春酒 3 月 4 日 (週五) 將辦在美食宮殿。我們會享用 10 道菜的中式宴席，有許多名菜，例如北京烤鴨和紅燒肉。晚上 6：30 開席上第一道菜，所以務必提早到達。

以下是表決結果。我們向無法出席的人致歉，希望明年春酒能看到你們。

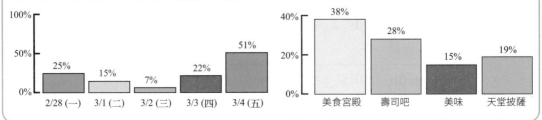

(B) 1.第一封信的主旨為何？

　　(A) 看誰能來，誰不能來。　　　　(B) 為聚餐日期和場地辦票選。

　　(C) 歡迎員工長假歸來。　　　　　(D) 通知員工聚餐日期和地點。

(D) 2.根據第二封信，大部分人偏好的聚餐日期和餐廳為何？

　　(A) 2/28 (週一)，壽司吧。　　　(B) 3/2 (週三)，美味。

　　(C) 3/3 (週四)，天堂披薩。　　　(D) 3/4 (週五)，美食宮殿。

(B) 3.下列關於春酒，下列敘述何者正確？

　　(A) 參加饗宴的員工可以拿紅包。

　　(B) 想出席的員工應通知人力資源部。

　　(C) 宴席會有 5 道菜，6：30 開席。

　　(D) 除北京烤鴨外和紅燒肉外，餐廳也提供素菜。

(D) 4.關於春酒聚餐投票，下列何者正確？

　　(A) 想吃壽司的員工最少。

　　(B) 選週四的員工多於四分之一。

　　(C) 披薩和壽司是兩個最熱門選擇。

　　(D) 多數員工不想要週三聚餐。

(C) 5.人力資源第二封信最後一句話的意思為何？

　　(A) 他們覺得抱歉，承諾給那些不能出席春酒聚餐的人小禮物。

　　(B) 他們將馬上策劃另一場春酒聚餐，給那些不能到的人。

　　(C) 春酒聚餐是一年一度活動。希望那些不能來的人，明年能夠到場。

　　(D) 明年仍會為春酒聚餐辦投票。希望所有的員工都還願意參加票選。

Pop Quiz

1. notified　　2. advance　　3. banquet　　4. annual　　5. apologized

Do You Know!?

常見的職務

HR (Human Resource)：人力資源　　PM (Project Manager)：專案經理

QA (Quality Assurance)：品質保證　　(Product Marketing)：產品行銷

Sales：業務　　　　　　　　　　　(Product Manager)：產品經理

電話留言

以下是兩張留言便箋。

留言對象： 羅傑	留言人： 戴夫	留言記錄： 卡羅 (#808)
分機號碼： #210	日期： 2/2	時間： 8:30 上午/ 下午

1. 戴夫的電腦自動關機，好幾個檔案消失不見。請檢測他的電腦，幫他修復那些消失的檔案。
2. 吉米今天休假一天。戴夫已傳送吉米今天應該給你的報告。請讓戴夫知道你有沒有收到檔案。
3. 戴夫想重新安排和你開會的時間。這週五不行，你下週一 (2/9) 早上 9 點或 10 點能和他碰面嗎？因為有個非常重要的客戶剛通知戴夫，這週五要見他。戴夫說他真心對此感到抱歉。

是否要求回電？ 是 / 否　　完成日期 / 時間　 2 / 2

留言對象： 戴夫	留言人： 羅傑	留言記錄： 艾瑪 (#215)
分機號碼： #812	日期： 2/2	時間： 4:30 上午 /下午

1. 羅傑明天早上會修你的電腦。他猜是你的硬碟壞掉了。他會嘗試修復你的檔案。然而，他無法保證所有的檔案都能復原。
2. 羅傑說，「多謝！」他收到報告了。然而，關於報告，他有些問題。他明天會直接問吉米。
3. 羅傑說，「不要緊。」他下週一早上 10 點沒問題。

是否要求回電？ 是 / 否　　完成日期 / 時間　 2 / 2

(D) 1. 這兩張便箋是什麼？

　　(A) 文字簡訊。　　　　　　　　(B) 電子郵件。

　　(C) 錄音留言。　　　　　　　　(D) 辦公室間電話留言。

(B) 2. 根據便箋，下列何者正確？

　　(A) 員工的上班時間很可能是朝九晚五。

　　(B) 艾瑪和戴夫可能在同一個部門。

　　(C) 戴夫必須回電給羅傑討論問題。

　　(D) 卡羅已回電給戴夫，但接電話的是艾瑪。

(A) 3.下列問題，何者未在便箋中被提及？

　　　⒜吉米的報告未送給羅傑。

　　　⒝戴夫的電腦當機，一些檔案不見了。

　　　⒞羅傑會打電話給吉米，也會問他關於報告的一些問題。

　　　⒟羅傑可能無法修復戴夫電腦上的檔案。

(D) 4.戴夫和羅傑何時開會？

　　　⒜下午 10:00，週一，2 月 2 日。　⒝上午 10:00，週二，2 月 3 日。

　　　⒞下午 10:00，週五，2 月 6 日。　⒟上午 10:00，週一，2 月 9 日。

(C) 5.羅傑的工作可能是下列何者？

　　　⒜會計師。　　　⒝祕書。　　　⒞電腦工程師。⒟保安。

▶ Pop Quiz

1. shuts　　2. guarantees　　3. genuinely　　4. accountant　　5. extension

Do You Know!?

常見的電話對話

表明身分：(This is) ○○○ (speaking / calling). 我是○○○。

詢問身問： 1. Excuse me, who is this? 不好意思，請問哪裡找？

　　　　　2. May I ask who is calling, please? 請問您是哪一位？

請○○○接聽： 1. May I have extension ○○○? 可以幫我轉分機○○○嗎？

　　　　　　2. May I speak to ○○○? 我可以跟○○○講話嗎？

轉接：I'll put you through. 我幫您轉接。

請稍後：Just a moment / minute.

別掛斷：Can you hold on a moment / hold the line?

無法接聽： 1.○○○ is not in / here (right now). ○○○(目前)不在。

　　　　　2.○○○ is out (at the moment). ○○○(目前)外出。

　　　　　3.○○○ is in a meeting. ○○○會議中。

留言：May I leave a message? (我可以留言嗎？)

打錯電話：Sorry, you have the wrong number. (抱歉，你打錯電話了。)

廣告和投訴函

以下是一則廣告和一封投訴函。

健美 X

推出新方法取得豐碩成果！

不到一個月就辦得到！

最新的健身器材創新力作 Acceletron，是一種肌肉刺激器，可以：

1.打造肌肉　　2.減重　　3.改善心臟功能　　4.增強體力　　5.提升體能

作用方式

Acceletron 肌肉刺激器利用發送小型電脈衝到你全身，刺激你的肌肉收縮。這些收縮類似於運動對你的身體造成的效果，但不會留下同樣的傷害。這讓你的肌肉能較快成長，而且能長時間勞動。

此外，已經證實，平均而言，Acceletron 一個月能幫你減去 10 磅。

收件人：	健美 X
寄件人：	約翰・哈曼
主旨：	退款要求

親愛的健美 X，

我兩個月前購買你們的 Acceletron 肌肉刺激器，想正式投訴此產品的品質。

首先，使用這項產品很痛苦。電擊經常造成我全身無法控制的亂動，非常的不舒服。其次，這項產品充電要花很久的時間。我經常必須等候 12 個小時，才能再度使用。最後也是最重要的，每日使用達一個月後，看不出肌肉量明顯增加或體重減少。你的產品似乎完全沒有效果。

我對你的產品極其失望，希望全額退款。

誠摯的，

約翰・哈曼

(B) 1.這個廣告的目的為何？

    (A) 雇用更多員工。   (B) 宣傳新商品。

    (C) 邀請顧客到新分店。   (D) 解釋新的先進科技。

(B) 2. Acceletron 肌肉刺激器如何增長肌肉？

    (A) 刺激心跳。   (B) 電擊肌肉。

    (C) 伸展肌肉以加速成長。   (D) 騙過大腦以增長肌肉。

(A) 3.約翰的投訴信未提及下列何者？

    (A) 器材太貴。   (B) 沒有達到預期效果。

    (C) 電擊不舒服。   (D) 為器材充電費時太久。

(D) 4.約翰希望獲得的補償為何？

    (A) 正式道歉。

    (B) 未來購物享折扣優惠。

    (C) 一個新的 Acceletron 肌肉刺激器。

    (D) 他購買的產品的退款。

(B) 5.第一段最可能在_____雜誌上看到。

    (A) 時尚和設計。   (B) 健身和養生。

    (C) 家庭和教育。   (D) 科學和環保。

Pop Quiz

1. apology   2. noticeable   3. objective   4. physical   5. overall

Do You Know!?

熱量 7700 大卡 = 1 公斤脂肪!?

如果消耗 7700 大卡就會減少一公斤的體重嗎？答案只對了一半！若只靠節食和以基礎代謝來減重，容易造成身體代謝變差、肌肉量減少。況且 100 大卡的蔬果和 100 大卡的炸雞為身體帶來的效益並不同。因此若想要減重不復胖，最好的辦法還是改變飲食習慣和增加運動量喔！

紅袋鼠

以下是一段有喬的學習筆記的文字。

紅袋鼠是體型最大的袋鼠，重可達 90 公斤，身高可達 2 公尺。

成年的公袋鼠叫做「巴克」(雄袋鼠)，成年的母袋鼠名叫「豆」(雌袋鼠)，小袋鼠是「揪伊」(幼袋鼠)。

紅袋鼠住在澳洲乾燥遼闊的平原上。牠們一般的跳躍移動速度約每小時 25 公里，但最快可達約每小時 70 公里 (並維持時速 40 公里連續跳約 2 公里遠)。牠們每跳一步，通常是 1.5 到 2 公尺遠。然而，當牠們全速前進，一跳就能超過 9 公尺，高度至 3 公尺。

世界紀錄
男子跳遠 8.95 公尺！
男子跳高 2.45 公尺！

紅袋鼠住在澳洲內陸大部分地區，很能適應沙漠地區的炎熱乾燥環境。如果有足夠的新鮮綠草可供食用，牠們完全不喝水也能存活。

「內陸」是一片覆蓋澳洲大部份的廣大區域。

(A) 1.本文主旨為何？

⒜ 紅袋鼠的簡介。

⒝ 住澳洲內陸的物種。

⒞ 比較袋鼠和人類的體力。

⒟ 紅袋鼠和其他袋鼠的不同之處。

(D) 2.根據本文，下列關於紅袋鼠的敘述，何者正確？

⒜ 紅袋鼠可能長到 3 公尺高。

⒝ 所有紅袋鼠的體重至少都有 90 公斤。

⒞ 紅袋鼠的自然棲息地因為氣候變遷正在縮減。

⒟ 全速前進時，紅袋鼠跳躍可以比人類跳遠世界紀錄更遠。

(B) 3.紅袋鼠如何能在沙漠地區炎熱乾燥的環境下存活？

(A) 牠們體內能儲水。

(B) 牠們吃新鮮的草就能得到足夠的水份。

(C) 牠們睡很久以保持涼爽。

(D) 牠們把自己埋進沙漠沙子裡，躲避高溫。

(D) 4.文字旁邊，寫了哪些筆記？

(A) 紅袋鼠的平均壽命。

(B) 紅袋鼠的交配習慣。

(C) 紅袋鼠的族群數量。

(D) 依據不同性別和年齡賦予紅袋鼠的名字。

(A) 5.下列何者可由本文推論得知？

(A) 澳洲內陸大部分地區是沙漠。

(B) 全速前進，紅袋鼠一日內便能穿越澳洲內陸。

(C) 比起喝水，紅袋鼠更愛鮮草。

(D) 不久的將來，紅袋鼠將因劣質的棲息地而瀕臨絕種。

➡ Pop Quiz

1. species　　2. adapt　　3. measuring　　4. gender　　5. habitats

Do You Know!?

吃袋鼠，救生態!?

「袋鼠」在澳洲被視為國寶，然而袋鼠數量暴增使當地生態嚴重失衡。為解決此嚴重的生態問題，澳洲生態學家呼籲民眾獵捕袋鼠，並以袋鼠肉代替牛肉食用。但許多當地人拒絕食用袋鼠肉，認為袋鼠是澳洲象徵。

天燈：不只是無害的樂趣

天燈是小型紙製熱氣球，於亞洲各地傳統節慶中使用。在中國和台灣，放天燈是元宵節重要活動，數千天燈同時點亮劃過夜空。然而，由於危及野生動物又可能引發火災，天燈正備受檢視。

雖然有文化意義，專家已經警告，掉落的天燈有引發火災的風險。在一個案例中，一個天燈造成英格蘭斯梅西克一家塑膠工廠起火。天燈落在工廠，引燃儲放在那裡的物料，造成大火災。超過 200 名消防隊到場滅火。

火災不是天燈引發的唯一問題。它們也可能傷到野生動物。牛隻死亡，因為天燈的金屬線落在牠們的飼料並造成牠們內部出血。一匹小馬必須安樂死，因為牠被掉下來的天燈驚嚇到，腿受重傷。

這類事件已激起全面禁售和禁放天燈的呼聲。現在，天燈在德國和奧地利都屬違法，澳洲的許多州也不准賣天燈，因為那裡引發叢林大火的風險太高。天燈可能看似無害，但它們有造成毀滅性大火、對野生動物形成嚴重威脅的潛在可能性。因此，我們必須採取行動解決問題，以免為時過晚。

(C) 1.本文主旨為何？

　　(A) 元宵節必備天燈。

　　(B) 消防人員成功撲滅由天燈引起的火災。

　　(C) 天燈威脅到環境和動物。

　　(D) 天燈的文化意義遠比潛在危險重要。

(B) 2.第二段的「點燃」所指為何？

　　(A) 掩蓋。

　　(B) 點著。

　　(C) 捏造。

　　(D) 擊倒。

(B) 3.為什麼澳洲有些州禁售天燈？

　　(A) 天燈殺了他們的牛。

　　(B) 天燈容易引起火災。

　　(C) 天燈落在他們的工廠上。

　　(D) 天燈使他們的馬受傷。

(D) 4.作者對天燈的態度為何？

    (A) 中立的。

    (B) 漠不關心的。

    (C) 支持的。

    (D) 反對的。

(A) 5.下一段最可能討論的主題為何？

    (A) 達到無天燈世界的方法。

    (B) 可應用在天燈上的新科技。

    (C) 更多關於天燈掉落造成破壞的案例。

    (D) 人類是否該保護野生動物和環境的辯論。

Pop Quiz

1. significance   2. banned   3. severely   4. motivated   5. Despite

Do You Know!?

環保天燈：讓環境保護與文化傳承並行

你是否也想親身體驗享譽國內外的平溪天燈節呢？但這項傳統文化所帶來的環境問題讓人很頭痛。臺灣非營利組織——文化銀行，為此研發讓環保與文化並存的「環保天燈」，一種材料能回歸山林的天燈。雖然目前環保天燈的造價很高，但期許未來每位到平溪的遊客可以藉由平價環保的方式傳承在地文化。

綠色產業研討會議程

守望地球的年度綠色產業研討會

系列講座將於 9/18 週一 09:00–16:00

廣場大旅館第二會議廳舉行

守望地球旨在協助各國政府和組織，藉由鼓勵基礎建設項目採用綠色選擇來降低環境衝擊。出席者將學習環保相關領域的各式各樣環保設備和管理方式。

議程

時間	會議室	講題和主講人
09:00–09:30	A	**開幕**——約瑟夫・山本 a. 介紹 b. 議程和目標概述
09:30–10:40	A	**水和廢水**——伊莉莎白・莫林 a. 垃圾處理和回收設備 b. 水處理 c. 純水處理
10:40–11:00	**休息時間**(走廊有簡單茶點招待)	
11:00–12:00	A	**汙水淤泥處理和回收**——卡爾・羅辛
	B	**空氣汙染防治**——馬丁・舒爾茲
12:00–13:30	**午餐**	
13:30–14:40	A	**垃圾管理和回收**——大衛・霍巴特
	B	**有機產品**——艾倫・海爾絲
14:40–15:00	**休息時間**(走廊有簡單茶點招待)	
15:00–16:00	A	**閉幕**——約瑟夫・山本 a. 問答時間 b. 抽獎 c. 下次研討會事項宣布

(C) 1. 這場研討會的主旨為何？

(A) 執法汙染控制法律。　　(B) 鼓勵公司栽種更多植物。

(C) 建議對環境友善的解決方案。　(D) 協助組織找到節能設備。

(B) 2.下列何者與第一段「綠色選擇」的意義最相近？

   (A) 基礎設施會被漆成綠色。

   (B) 基礎設施能有助保護環境。

   (C) 政府必須興建公園做為綠色基礎設施。

   (D) 如果你是出席者之一，大家會嫉妒。

(C) 3.出席者在研討會中有幾次休息時間？

   (A) 1。　　　　(B) 2。　　　　(C) 3。　　　　(D) 4。

(D) 4.研討會結束時，下列何者不正確？

   (A) 出席者可以提問。

   (B) 主持人將介紹下次研討會。

   (C) 出席者有機會贏得獎品。

   (D) 所有出席者都將獲贈免費禮品。

(D) 5.王先生對天然食品感興趣，他應該參加下列哪個場次？

   (A) 11:00–12:00，會議室 A。　　　(B) 11:00–12:00，會議室 B。

   (C) 13:30–14:40，會議室 A。　　　(D) 13:30–14:40，會議室 B。

Pop Quiz

1. enforce　　2. organic　　3. objective　　4. recycled　　5. pollution

Do You Know!?

透過綠色產業，讓臺灣這塊土地更好。

國際綠色產業聯合會 (International Green Industry Union) 認為 「在生產過程中，基於環保考慮，藉助科技，以綠色生產機制力求在資源使用上節約以及汙染減少的產業」即為綠色產業。而臺灣其中一個案例為雲林成龍村的白蝦養殖。為了不讓超抽地下水造成地層下陷，政府鼓勵當地漁民使用龍鬚菜淨化水質，設計出能夠自給自足的魚塭，讓原先面臨地層下陷危機的小漁村，在綠色產業中找到新出路。

大淨灘

以下是一張傳單和一則新聞。

我們來淨灘

西田沙灘協會將於 6 月 8 日舉行淨灘活動。我們希望辦成我們歷來最大規模淨灘活動，所以請帶幾位朋友或家人來參加——老少均可，沒有關係！

今年，查理貝果咖啡店贊助我們淨灘，將提供我們咖啡和貝果，讓我們勇往直前。請自備可重覆使用的杯子和盤子來。

何不參加我們的淨灘比賽呢？四人一組，各組比賽看誰收集到最多的垃圾。贏家將獲得有趣的神祕禮物！請幫我們把淨灘的消息傳遞出去。到時見！

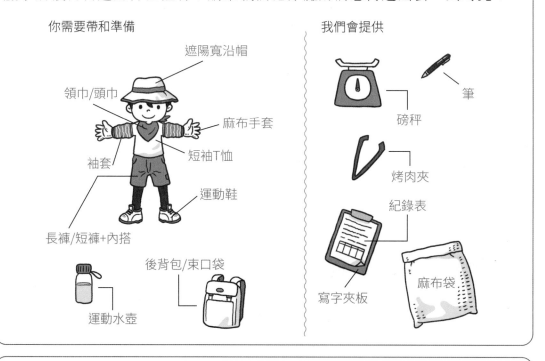

你需要帶和準備

遮陽寬沿帽
領巾/頭巾
麻布手套
短袖T恤
袖套
運動鞋
長褲/短褲+內搭
後背包/束口袋
運動水壺

我們會提供

筆
磅秤
烤肉夾
紀錄表
寫字夾板
麻布袋

(西田太陽報)——好幾十名志工昨天聚集在西田沙灘，參加年度淨灘活動。西田沙灘協會負責人凱特·伊凡斯估計，共收集到將近半公噸的垃圾。伊凡斯說：「事實上比去年垃圾少很多，我們大感欣慰。我們的長期目標是教育民眾，一開始就別把垃圾留在沙灘。這個訊息似乎傳達開了。」 天氣很涼爽，有風，超過百人現身參加活動。「我們很高興這麼多人現身。有全家都來的，從老奶奶到小朋友，撿拾垃圾並享受美好時光。真是棒透了！」伊凡斯說。

（ A ）1.傳單的主旨為何？

　　　(A) 鼓勵大家出席活動。　　　　　　(B) 強調家庭的重要性。

　　　(C) 邀請公司贊助活動。　　　　　　(D) 提高公眾對環境保護的認知。

（ B ）2.根據傳單，下列何者是淨灘志工被要求隨身攜帶的東西？

　　　(A) 點心。　　　　(B) 手套。　　　(C) 垃圾袋。　　　(D) 記錄表。

（ A ）3.為什麼志工被要求帶可重覆使用的杯盤？

　　　(A) 他們會獲得免費食物和飲料。　(B) 他們可以借此收集更多垃圾。

　　　(C) 他們將回收杯盤。　　　　　　(D) 他們需要杯盤以進入比賽。

（ C ）4.新聞中的「訊息」所指為何？

　　　(A) 淨灘是很棒的活動。

　　　(B) 歡迎大家前來參加淨灘。

　　　(C) 大家不該將垃圾留在沙灘上。

　　　(D) 各個家庭一起撿垃圾，其樂融融。

（ C ）5.下列關於今年淨灘活動的敘述，何者正確？

　　　(A) 小朋友不准參加此項活動。　　(B) 參加活動的不足 100 人。

　　　(C) 志工有茶點招待。　　　　　　(D) 志工被要求繳交入場費。

▶ Pop Quiz

1. delighted　　2. estimated　　3. volunteer　　4. contest　　5. sponsored

Do You Know!?

太平洋垃圾帶——海上垃圾島

位於副熱帶高壓帶的北太平洋環流系統是海洋中相對靜止的區域。海中的垃圾透過洋流運送堆積於此，形成一個約有兩個美國面積大的垃圾帶，學者估計垃圾重量超過一億噸。垃圾帶中多為塑膠廢物，除了危害海洋生物外，經分解後的垃圾經層層食物鏈，最終還是會回到人類身上。為了海洋生態，也為了自己的健康，大家一起減塑生活吧！

協助我們拯救我們的海洋

以下是兩封信件。

收件人：	海洋生物學系
寄件人：	拯救我們的海洋
主旨：	邀請您來漁業資源枯竭講座

親愛的海洋生物學系，

誠摯邀請您來聽有關濫捕導致我們的海洋漁業資源逐漸枯竭的系列講座。

在活動期間，我們打算探討過度捕撈的問題，對這個日益嚴重的隱憂，提出可能的解決方案。我們希望，您出席我們的研討會，能以某種方式協助守護我們珍貴海洋的抗爭，讓每個人的未來都更好。

我們的第一位講者是大衛·霍夫曼，海洋生態管理領域的專家，他將詳細闡述自 1980 年代以來魚類數量發生的變化。 我們第二天的講者是吉兒·艾勃納西，她會討論漁撈規定和執法相關問題。第三天也是最後一位講者是喬治·波格特，河流暨海洋保護委員會的主席。他將談必須做哪些事，以確保未來有永續發展的漁業。

時間和日期：9:00–12:00, 3/12–3/14　　地點：紅龍飯店，四廳
票價：單張門票　　　台幣 150 元 (任選一場演講)
　　　雙張套票　　　台幣 250 元 (任選兩場演講)
　　　全套門票　　　台幣 300 元 (出席全部三場演講)

線上訂票請至 www.saveouroceans.com/eventbookings
(所有出席者都必須事先預約。)

如有任何問題，請告知我們。

引頸期盼的，
拯救我們的海洋　　　　　　　　　　　　　　聯絡電話：(02)1234–5678

收件人：	拯救我們的海洋
寄件人：	辛西雅
主旨：	詢問單場門票

親愛的拯救我們的海洋，

我們對研討會很感興趣，想下單買票。我們需要單場門票，粗估約 100–120 張。請告知你們能提供多少座位。此外，我們想知道你們能否提供特別折扣。

期待聽到你們的消息。

誠摯的，
辛西雅
海洋生物系助理

(B) 1.根據第一封電子郵件，演講的主旨為何？

　　(A) 生物學。　　(B) 過度漁撈。　　(C) 海洋生物。　　(D) 捕魚法規。

(D) 2.第二封電子郵件的主旨為何？

　　(A) 要求退款。　　　　　　　　(B) 提出投訴。

　　(C) 提出關於捕魚建議。　　　　(D) 詢問更多資訊。

(A) 3.第一封電子郵件裡「日益嚴重的隱憂」，所指為何？

　　(A) 魚類資源減少。　　　　　　(B) 聽講觀眾缺席。

　　(C) 漁船造成的海洋汙染。　　　(D) 改革漁撈規定的問題。

(B) 4.下列關於此項活動的敘述，何者不正確？

　　(A) 這場活動持續三天。　　　　(B) 可以現場買票。

　　(C) 由環保組織主辦。　　　　　(D) 演講都從九點開始，中午結束。

(C) 5.下列何者可由第二段推論得知？

　　(A) 辛西雅謝絕參加研討會。

　　(B) 辛西雅想要立刻獲得回覆。

　　(C) 辛西雅希望以較低價格買到門票。

　　(D) 辛西雅確定有足夠座位容納 100 人。

➡ Pop Quiz

1. regulations　　2. elaborate　　3. granted　　4. Marine　　5. ensure

Do You Know!?

慢魚運動 Slow Fish Event

義大利的慢魚運動，主張以慢捕、慢食改變海洋生態。慢魚運動讓人們懂得魚的故事，吃當地、當季的新鮮魚貨，而非吃特定魚類。四面環海的臺灣漁獲數量每況愈下，我們或許也該借鏡慢魚運動，一步步改變海洋生態。

能自稀薄空氣製水的看板

有什麼比一杯清涼潔淨的飲用水更好？那一杯由廣告看板製作出來的清涼潔淨飲用水如何呢？對，你沒看錯。

在秘魯利馬，有一種新設計出來的廣告看板，確實是從稀薄空氣裡捉取水分。像三明治一樣被夾在廣告看板中間的是一組複雜的高科技過濾系統。

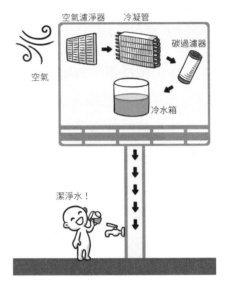

第一階段，當風吹過這個廣告看板時，一個空氣濾淨器移除空氣中的雜質。然後空氣經由連串的冷凝管冷卻，使得空氣裡的水集結成大顆水滴，道理就像雨水形成一樣。這些水通過一個碳過濾器後，收集在冷水箱裡。接下來，重力帶著水流下水管，到靠近地面的水龍頭。

這個廣告看板每天收集超過 100 公升的水，在年降雨量不到 0.5 英吋的城市，提供迫切需要的飲用水。

此區獨特的地理條件能解釋其雨水匱乏。利馬西邊就是太平洋，這表示空氣非常潮溼。然而利馬以北是地表最乾燥的沙漠之一。利馬有逾 120 萬人沒有自來水，所以廣告看板提供了人們想取得潔淨便宜飲用水的夢想或許指日可待。

(A) 1. 作者對高科技廣告看板的態度為何？

  (A) 有信心的。   (B) 漠不關心的。

  (C) 有敵意的。   (D) 多疑的。

(D) 2. 為什麼作者在第一段說：「對，你沒看錯。」？

  (A) 嘲笑讀者蹩腳的閱讀技巧。

  (B) 教讀者有關廣告看板的基本事項。

  (C) 鼓勵大家質疑自己看到的每件事。

  (D) 強調廣告看板能製作飲用水。

(C) 3. 根據本文，廣告看板收集到的水來自何處？

  (A) 雲。   (B) 內陸河。

  (C) 潮溼空氣。   (D) 大西洋。

(B) 4.儲存到冷水箱之前，水在最後階段發生了什麼事？

      (A) 溫度降低。

      (B) 通過碳過濾器。

      (C) 和純淨雨水混和。

      (D) 分解成微小粒子。

(A) 5.本文最後一句話，作者所指為何？

      (A) 利馬的人可能很快就能取得便宜的飲用水。

      (B) 我們永遠不該低估創意思考的力量。

      (C) 更多高科技廣告看板正在設立，但需要更多的投資。

      (D) 氣候變遷快速，所以我們必須在為時已晚之前做點事。

Pop Quiz

1. literally   2. carbon   3. hostile   4. investment   5. underestimated

Do You Know!?

新加坡的四個水龍頭 (Four Taps)

新加坡的「四個水龍頭」代表四項水策略，分別是輸入水、在地水源、淡化水及高度淨化水。前兩項為目前多國所使用。新加坡人最自豪其淡化、淨化水源的技術。新加坡透過淡化海水、淨化回收水技術生產出的新生水 (NEWater) 目前已經供應新加坡三成以上用水，並持續穩定的成長中。他們的造水技術漸漸讓新加坡人遠離水源短缺的困境。

靜水谷急迫的安全隱憂

經濟部中央地質調查所已公布令人意外的發現。調查顯示靜水谷 30% 的土地有土壤液化風險。

土壤液化是潮溼土壤碰到突發的外力作用，例如遇到地震時，會像液體一樣流動的狀態。通常，當土壤被建築物的重量擠壓時，壓力會引發地下水流至表層。然而，如果地表劇烈、突發或反覆震動，水沒有時間流走，土壤顆粒就會鬆動。這種鬆動導致土壤像液體般流動，讓地表很不穩定。

都市地區土壤液化的後果，從道路和基礎建設輕微受損，到大樓倒塌都可能。因此，這是政府需優先處理的議題。

靜水谷特別容易發生土壤液化，因為河水使土壤含水飽和。那裡的土壤顆粒也特別細，進一步提高土壤液化的可能性。這對住在這些高風險區的人形成安全問題。

即便如此，東邊的住宅區相對安全；最大隱憂是北邊工業區伯斯伍德，那裡風險最高。該區的火力發電廠是整個城市的主要供電來源，所以面對土壤液化，這個城市很可能停電長達數週或甚至數月。

高危險區
居民應即刻尋找專業技師檢測評估大樓地基。

中危險區
居民可以下載自我評估表檢查大樓安全。

低危險區
無須擔心。

火力發電廠　工廠　住宅

塔拉河　艾治薑德區　伯斯伍德區　諾里奇區　約克區　中央區　金斯利區

N

(D) 1.土壤液化的意義為何？

　　　(A) 土壤與雪混和後變成泥。

　　　(B) 土壤因建築物的重量擠壓而增加強度。

　　　(C) 多數又大又重的建築物遇地震容易倒塌。

　　　(D) 地下水流不到表層，讓土壤如液體般流動。

(C) 2. 為什麼土壤液化對靜水谷是嚴重威脅？

      (A) 這裡有大片工業區。　　　　(B) 建築物蓋得差。

      (C) 這裡是地質敏感區。　　　　(D) 政府沒有積極做事。

(C) 3. 下列何者沒有土壤液化風險？

      (A) 約克區。　　　　　　　　(B) 中央區。

      (C) 諾里奇區。　　　　　　　(D) 伯斯伍德區。

(A) 4. 下列何者可由地圖推論得知？

      (A) 塔拉河流過約克區和中央區。

      (B) 大部分居民住約克區和金斯利區。

      (C) 工廠大多設在艾治華德區和中央區。

      (D) 伯斯伍德區的居民不必擔心土壤液化。

(D) 5. 下列何者可由本文推論得知？

      (A) 地震來襲時，本市可能淹水。

      (B) 住在高風險區的人一定要立刻搬到較安全地區。

      (C) 住在中風險區的人不必擔心。

      (D) 地震來襲時，本市可能停電。

➤ Pop Quiz

1. likelihood　　2. economic　　3. collapsed　　4. consequences　　5. moderate

Do You Know!?

做好準備，土壤液化不可怕

面對土壤液化時，不需過於恐慌。除了位於土壤液化高潛勢區之外，也必須同時滿足砂質土層、高地下水位及強烈地震這三大要素，才有立即危險。另外，即使液化發生，有數層地下室及深地基的高樓不會造成太大影響。而低矮樓房也僅是傾斜，大多不會傾倒造成生命危險。與其害怕土壤液化，更應重視建築物結構及安全性，以避免地震時造成的人員傷亡。

Cloze Test
—克漏字與文意選填

劉美皇／編著

本書特色：

1. 精選35篇英語短文，題材豐富多元。

2. 結合克漏字及文意選填兩種大考題型，使學習相輔相成、事半功倍。

3. 完整的文法與延伸整理，提供有效率的深入學習。

4. 獨創字彙跑馬燈，生難字詞一目了然。

5. 隨書附精闢解析與文章中譯，教師課堂教學或學生自我練習皆適用。

6. 團體訂購附贈隨堂評量。

大考三題型：
克漏字&文意選填&篇章結構

簡薰育／編著

大考關鍵三題型，一本就搞定！

對克漏字、文意選填及篇章結構
感到恐懼？

你，缺的就是這一本！

本書特色：

1. 收錄20回克漏字、15回文意選填及15回篇章結構，紮實訓練大考關鍵
   三題型！
2. 測驗題符合大考命題原則及出題走向，著重測驗文意理解。
3. 每回皆含翻譯練習，累積翻譯及寫作實力。
4. 精選字彙補充，複習大考重要字彙與其用法。

學校團體訂購附贈8回隨堂評量。

指考篇章・閱測秘技

王靖賢、蘇文賢／編著

本書特色：

1. 本書包含理論篇和題目篇。理論篇精闢分析文章架構、學習如何抓出文章重點及關鍵字，迅速瞭解文章結構、掌握答題技巧。

2. 題目篇收錄20則篇章結構和20則閱讀測驗文章，內容多元豐富，囊括各類題材，讓您熟練各類主題。

3. 解析本含全文中譯及各題詳解。

關於 Reading Power

這是一套為愉閱英語而生，

一套能體驗英閱樂趣，

本書依據教育部提出之性別平等、人權、環境、海洋教育等多項議題撰寫 36 回仿大考、英檢及多益閱讀測驗文章。文章揉合各式各樣閱讀媒材、模式，讓你在攻克英文閱讀測驗同時也能閱讀生活中的英文。

本書特色：

✔ 多元的閱讀素材，如傳單、信件、海報等，一網打盡各項測驗的閱測文章。

✔ 彙整單篇、雙篇與多篇的閱讀模式符合各項英文測驗趨勢！

✔ 每篇搭配 5 題閱讀測驗試題，讓你對英文閱讀測驗更得心應手。

✔ 貼心整理文章生難字及例句，搭配 5 題 Pop Quiz，單字學習沒問題。

解析本：

✔ 附文章、題目中譯與解答，讓你輕鬆學習無負擔。

✔ 精心規劃 Do You Know!? 專欄，讓你學習英文之餘，補充趣味小知識。

✔ 學校團體訂購附 8 回贈卷。

一套能開拓視野見聞，

一套能厚植英語實力，

一套讓人愛不釋手的系列叢書。

「英閱百匯」與「解析本」不分售
97-80454G

三民網路書店
www.sanmin.com.tw